CHORUS OF ASHES

THE WILDSONG SERIES
BOOK 3

TRICIA O'MALLEY

LOVEWRITE PUBLISHING

CHORUS OF ASHES
THE WILDSONG SERIES
BOOK THREE

"Storms make trees take deeper roots."
    Dolly Parton

The Fae Realm

Danula

The Light Fae ruled by the Goddess Danu

The Elemental Fae

The Royal Fae Court of the Danula oversee
the Elemental Fae

Water Fae

Earth Fae   Fire Fae

Air Fae

Domnua

The Dark Fae ruled by Goddess Domnu

PROLOGUE

"What say you, Rian?"

"I've never lain with this woman. You are judging the wrong person. I stand by my innocence." Rian's heart hammered in his chest, and he narrowed his eyes at the crowd, searching for anything unusual. Did the true culprit lie hidden in the audience, watching as the High Court of the Danula Fae handed down a sentence to an innocent man?

His own people had turned on him.

Rian, as head of magicks training for the Earth Fae, was standing trial for allegedly having an affair with the wife of one of the Royal Fae. It wasn't true, not even close, and the unfairness of the situation he now found himself in made his stomach burn. It was a wrongdoing to lay with another's fated mate, and the crime was often punishable by the stripping of one's powers. However, when it came to the royals, the price was much higher.

Exile.

Now, Rian faced having to leave his family, his homeland, and his people – all because someone had supposedly seen him near the royal's home when the crime was discovered. The evidence was tenuous at best, and Rian wanted to scream as the supposed witness stood up before the court.

The hearing took place deep in the bowels of the castle of the Danula Fae, the rulers of the various factions of the Elemental Fae, so that should any punishment need to be administered quickly, the convicted would have no option for escape. White marble walls with no windows, high ceilings, and gleaming gold light fixtures highlighted the starkness of the room. Long benches lay in three rows in front of a large gold table where the judging committee met to overhear cases. Rian's eyes lit on one woman in the audience, and his breath caught in his throat.

She was furiously, stunningly beautiful.

And if looks could kill, well, Rian would be eviscerated on the spot.

A hammered gold circlet of leaves held back shining brown curls that tumbled over her shoulders, and green silk caressed her softly curved body. Eyes the color of her dress glared at him, and Rian could feel her anger from across the room. Judged and found guilty, Rian realized. It was a good thing this woman wasn't on the committee, or he'd likely be put to his death.

She was Terra, leader of the Earth Fae, and Rian had only ever seen her from afar. Unlike other factions of Fae, where rulers were ever present in daily life, Terra took a more nuanced approach, preferring to lead with a soft touch from the forests that surrounded their castle. She wasn't one for pomp and circumstance, and now, seeing how she commanded attention even while sitting silently in the audience, Rian understood that he'd grossly underestimated the power she wielded. He wondered who this royal philanderer was to her.

A sob drew his attention, and his stomach twisted. Rian's mother sat, her arms clutched around her frail body, tears streaming down her cheeks. While she believed his story, wholeheartedly, they both understood that the royals always got what they wanted. Whatever secretive agenda was at play here would unfold as they saw fit, no matter what lives they sacrificed in doing so. Rage slid more deeply through him, becoming sinister and dark, as he was commanded to stand.

"Any final words, Rian, Ruler of Magicks?" This from the head of council, a man that Rian did not know, whose face remained placid as though he was asking after the weather.

"I did not commit this crime you've accused me of. I'm an honest man, a proud Earth Fae, and I live a humble life in service to my mother. I'm all she has, you understand. I would never do anything to jeopardize my position in caring for her." Rian infused his voice with sincerity, though the sticky anger that clung to him made him want to shout. "There is no crime to be walking down a street at night. You've accused the wrong man, and I beg of you to reconsider your accusations ... or..."

"Or what?" The council leader raised his chin, a considering light in his eyes.

"You'll regret the day you exiled the wrong man." The anger won out, and a frigid wave swept the room at his words, causing the crowd to gasp as a sheet of ice coated the gold high table. Rian saw his mother close her eyes, and he knew, in that moment, that he'd let his emotions decide his future. Perhaps if he had managed to hide the level of his powers, or the depth of his rage, he would have walked out a free man.

Tempering who he was had never been his strong suit.

"We don't take kindly to threats." The council leader sniffed and turned to the others, who all nodded their heads. "Rian, Earth Fae and Ruler of Magicks, you are found guilty and exiled from our lands at once. You may have a moment to say goodbye to your mother."

Iron cuffs slipped around his wrists, binding his magick and stinging his skin. Rian didn't care about the burn, no, it was the only thing he could feel at the moment as his anger threatened to overtake him. A guard stepped forward and took his arm, drawing him from the stand and toward his mother.

"Rian." Aster, a slim woman with steely determination, wrapped her arms around him. As her tears soaked his tunic, Rian's heart broke into a thousand pieces only to be soldered with ice. Aster was sick, and they both knew this was more than a goodbye-for-now.

This would be the last time he saw his mother alive.

"I will avenge this," Rian whispered into her hair, pressing a kiss to the top of her head.

"Don't, Rian. For what purpose? I'll be..." Aster lifted tired eyes to his. "Promise me you'll seek your happiness. Wherever you land. There's more to this world than the Fae realms, and you may very well live a happy and fulfilled life elsewhere. Promise me you'll try."

"I ... how can I make that promise? This is wrong. What they're doing is *wrong*," Rian protested.

"And I'll continue to fight for you here, darling. I won't let this go, and if it's the last thing I do ... I'll try to get you home. But in the meantime, I can't... I can't go on if I know you're unhappy. You've always been a bright boy, strong, and you've brought so much joy to my life. Promise me you'll try?" Aster clung to him as the guard tugged his arm.

"I... I promise, Mother. I'll do my best to find happiness." *Which will come from seeking vengeance.* He bit his tongue as his mother leaned up to press a kiss to his cheek.

"May love carry you in strength," Aster whispered.

"May love carry you in strength," Rian repeated. The guard pulled him away.

"Rian," Aster said. He turned, his eyes locking on hers.

"Where the sun shines through the trees, blessing the ground with light, I will always be. Remember me, and I will come to you."

Rian nodded, shuttering his eyes against the tears that threatened. The unfairness of his situation slapped at his sense of justice. He'd always believed the Danula Fae to be fair rulers, and now he couldn't wrap his head around what was happening to him. The guard pulled him through a narrow door that led to a secondary room where the council waited.

Where *she* waited.

Rian's chin came up when his eyes landed on Terra. She met his challenging look with a smile. It seared him, melting some of the ice, only to allow his rage to flood through.

"You smile for the fate of an innocent," Rian spat.

"Justice is served." Terra shrugged a shoulder. "Breaking a fated mate bond brings great harm to not only the immediate family, but to the rules of our society. There is no stronger bond than that of fated mates."

"If she was bonded, then why was she lying with another man? Did you ever think to accuse *her* instead of her lover?" Rian grit out as the guard pulled him past Terra.

"Enough." The head council member thundered.

"I will avenge this wrongdoing. Of this, I promise you." Rian spoke to Terra.

A considering look entered Terra's eyes, but Rian was already being forced into a narrow corridor. The last thing he saw was Terra opening her mouth to speak, when the door slammed shut, and his world went black.

1

THREE YEARS LATER

"I SAY WE FIGHT."

Terra raised her eyes to where King Callum paced in front of the stream, his wife Lily having instead chosen to sit with Terra in the soft moss that coated the gently curved riverbank. The King of the Danula Fae's shoulders were rigid with tension, and she appreciated him meeting her out here instead of inside the castle. Walls made her feel like she wanted to bounce out of her skin, and she much preferred conducting business beneath the sky where the wind blew their words into the ether.

"But how? Are we aware of any organized advancing armies?" Terra asked. "Thus far, the Domnua Fae have been insidious in their actions, and all we've been able to do is react. Unless you choose to go to their realm?"

"We might have to." King Callum whirled, his hands at his hips, his face stormy.

"Our people are restless," Terra said, threading her fingers through the springy moss, feeling the worries of her people communicating through the roots in the Earth. "They know of the attacks on the Fire and Water Fae, and now look at each other with suspicion. We don't know if a Domnua has infiltrated our midst. What's their end game? Can we cut them off there?"

"It's Domnu," Lily, a lovely human who'd had the unusual good luck of being King Callum's fated mate, murmured. "The Dark Goddess will never rest until she can leave her realm and rule Ireland ... if not the Earth. Essentially, she's a toddler having one big tantrum. She doesn't like being told what to do, and she certainly doesn't want to compromise. Even though she's been given her own realm to rule, it's not enough. It will never be enough."

"But you can't *kill* a goddess," Terra protested.

"We can contain her. We can weaken her. We can take her powers from her." King Callum ticked the points off on his fingers.

"So the option to fight is to capture the Goddess Domnu?" Worry creased Lily's forehead. "Surely there's a better route?"

"Can we turn her people against her? Maybe show the Dark Fae how nice it is over here?" Terra mused.

"That would take a massive campaign that I'm not sure we have time for. All they know is Goddess Domnu as their leader. I'm not sure we'll have the strength to change that." King Callum crouched by Lily and pressed an absent-minded kiss to her forehead. Lily's eyes softened, and Terra couldn't help but smile in the presence of their love. Their love story had been fraught with danger and troubles but, somehow, they'd still found their way back to each other.

Terra suspected her own would be much the same. Her heart twisted as she thought about her fated mate, the man who'd been shown to her through the scrying stream. If it was the same man she thought it to be, well, it wasn't likely she'd be finding her happily-ever-after anytime soon.

Exiled.

In an awful twist of fate, Terra had heard her fated mate singing their heartsong in her dreams one night. It was the first time she'd heard their song, and when she'd awoken, excitement coursing through her body, she'd hurried to the stream to finally get a look at her mate. Her excitement had quickly shifted to dismay when the clear waters of the stream had shimmered to reveal her sworn enemy.

The man who had torn her family apart.

Bitterness filled her mouth as she thought about the aftermath of Rian's trial, his exile, and how her brother, Eoghan, had fallen apart at his fated mate's betrayal. Not only had his heart been broken, but the breaking of a fated mate bond had sent confusion and uncertainty through her people in a time when they needed to rely on consistency and foundational truths.

For the Fae, a fated mate was a singular truth that defined the course of one's life. The magick was so powerful, that once two Fae claimed each other and accepted their fated bond, not only did their own magicks grow stronger, but that of the entire community of Fae as a whole. If one Fae claimed their fated mate, and the other refused, the first Fae would eventually die from the unrequited claim.

A bit archaic, Terra supposed, as she'd often chafed against the confines of the fated mate expectations of the Earth Fae, instead largely enjoying her life untethered to another. Who said she needed a partner to be happy? She hadn't always thought that way, but watching Eoghan unravel at his wife's unfaithfulness had started her down a path of convincing herself that perhaps fated mates were an outdated and unnecessary construct.

Until she looked at Lily and Callum, that is. Terra's heart twisted, and a soft sigh escaped as Lily traced her finger over Callum's lips, unspoken words drifting between them. And then there were these two. Their bond was so strong, Terra could all but see the golden tendrils linking them together.

It would never be this way for her, Terra reminded herself, because her fated mate was exiled and an adulterer. Her choices were limited in the matter. Ignore his heartsong and continue to lead her people in the battle against the Dark Fae or leave their realm and live in exile with a man who had a deeply questionable moral compass.

The Fates certainly enjoyed their whims, did they not?

Except when it came to these two. Terra smiled indulgently at the lovers, happy they had found each other. Just because it wasn't written in the stars for her to have the same bond, didn't mean she begrudged anyone their happiness. Joy was something to be celebrated in any form.

"Well, I did find something..." Lily said shyly as she glanced from Callum to Terra. Though she'd proven herself to be a strong woman, Lily still was timid when it came to offering her insights on the Fae realm. Terra certainly couldn't blame her. The Fae were a mercurial and tricky lot, and their rules and history were a morass of riddles shrouded in mystery. "Perhaps it's nothing."

"Tell us, love. What did that sharp brain of yours dig out? Spending more time in the library were you?" Callum's eyes gleamed as he studied Lily.

"I was. Bianca and I can hardly tear ourselves away now that we have access to all this fascinating knowledge. It's, well, sure and it could take ages to read it all, couldn't it? But we did stumble on a little tidbit yesterday that we both think might be worth exploring." Lily tucked a stray tendril of warm brown hair behind her ear and pursed her lips. "It seems that while, yes, you are correct that we can't kill a goddess, you can incapacitate her."

"Is that right?" Callum's expression went from soft and loving to sharp and deadly in an instant.

"Bianca thinks it is why the Domnua are trying to divide us. It takes all of the Elementals to come together and work the spell that will strip Domnu of her powers."

"And if we unite? The ritual will require sacrifice, will it not?" Terra was well versed in the way of magicks. Nothing in this realm or the next came for free, and the energy they used here would be taken from something else.

"I believe so. But Bianca is digging more deeply today. You know how she is…" Lily laughed. Terra had only met Bianca recently, a human gifted magick from the Fae for her service in the battle of the Four Treasures, and she had recognized a kindred spirit instantly.

"That's great news. If anything, it gives us some direction. I'll admit, I'm frustrated. I hate being reactive and, after they took my mother, well, I'm ready for a fight." King Callum stood, his fists balled at his side. Immediately, Lily rose and wrapped her arms around his waist, leaning into him.

"Oh, we'll fight," Terra assured her king. "Of that I am certain. No longer can we ignore the cries of our people. The Domnua are insidious, and though every pest serves a purpose, at best, theirs is only to be an agent of change. Change for a better and brighter future for our world. To that end, I will commit."

"We'll reconvene tomorrow." King Callum gave her a nod, and Lily waved shyly at Terra as he tugged her toward the castle.

Turning, Terra wandered along the stream, the chill of the air nothing more than the brush of a lover's touch against her skin. Once she'd slipped deeper into the forest, she tugged her dress over her head, preferring to be naked among the trees. Here, she was home. Who needed a fated mate when she had the soft caress of the wind filtering through the leaves or the cool brush of icy water from a bubbling brook? Her heart belonged here, in the wilds, and she'd die protecting it.

A sharp warning from a small bird perched above her was the only alert she had. Whirling, Terra already had her knife in hand when the trio of Domnua met her on the path. The knife, the Earth Fae's amulet, was always strapped to her leg even when she went sky clad. An item of great importance, only those worthy of ruling their people could carry it. Now, Terra wielded it with grace, the blade fitting neatly into her palm as though it was carved for her and waited for the Domnua to make a move.

"Dirt wench." One of the Domnua hissed at her. Terra supposed that was his stab at an insult to the Earth Fae. The ground rumbled beneath her feet, signaling that her people were coming to her rescue, but Terra wouldn't need them.

She didn't like to kill but would do so when necessary.

In this case, it was necessary. Her blade was already slicing through the abdomen of the first Dark Fae that launched himself before she pivoted and took out the other two. They were no match for the strength of her talisman, for her blade was charged with the power of all of the Earth Fae. Even as the trees swayed and her people crept from the mists that clung to the forest floor, Terra was waving them back. Sheathing her blade, she took a deep breath.

Kneeling to where the Domnua were now only puddles of silvery blood, Terra began the last rites.

For even the darkest of souls needed to be sent home with care.

2

"RIAN, LAD, WHAT A NIGHT!" Cillian, Rian's second-in-command dropped onto the leather couch in the VIP section of the swanky gentlemen's club in Dublin. He tapped his whiskey glass against Rian's and took a sip, his eyes tracking the half-dressed waitresses walking around the club taking orders from the patrons. "I think that redhead is interested in you."

"Is she?" Rian studied one of the waitresses who kept shooting glances his way. It wasn't unusual for women to be interested in him. His Fae magick, though hidden to humans, still held a subtle whiff of otherness that apparently was intoxicating for many women. He'd grown jaded over the past few years, never having to put any effort into finding a lover willing to bed him, and now he turned away from the soft smile that promised more. His phone buzzed, and he answered it without justifying his dismissal of the redhead. "Rian here."

Rian listened to his project manager, one tasked with overseeing the removal of large swathes of the rain forest in order to plant commercial crops, ramble on about an orangutan family in the direct path of the bulldozers. Worry for the animals slipped through him, but he shut it down, building the icy wall around his heart that he'd done such a good job of maintaining over the past few years on his campaign to destroy the Earth. If he couldn't take his vengeance out on the Earth Fae directly, he'd do so by destroying the environment they cherished. Passive aggressive? Perhaps. But Rian took his revenge where he could. When his mother had died, alone, and he'd been unable to be there for her in her last days, Rian had stopped caring about the damage his actions caused.

At least that's what he told himself.

"Relocate them," Rian ordered, and hung up the phone. He couldn't bring himself to outright order the killing of the orangutans, because his Earth Fae roots were deeply engrained, but he was fine with destroying their home. His home had been ripped from him too. They'd adapt, much like he had, right? Though worry twisted low in his gut, along with an icky spread of self-loathing, Rian shoved the feelings away. Slamming his glass of whiskey, Rian poured himself another from the bottle at the table, ignoring the waitress who hurried over to do the task for him.

Revenge was all that mattered. He'd been wronged, and the Earth Fae would pay, one way or another.

"Problems?" Cillian asked. He'd pulled one woman onto his lap, cradling her at his waist, and raised an eyebrow at Rian. A part of Rian wished he had the easy confidence of Cillian, a man who cared only about money and the next woman who'd take him to bed.

While Rian played the same game, his heart wasn't in it. He hoped that with a few more years in this lifestyle, he'd eventually be able to shed any sense of remorse or empathy that he had for his actions. At the moment, regret and bitterness were his constant companions, along with the single-minded determination to make the Earth Fae rue the day they'd wrongly accused him and sent him into exile.

He'd landed in Ireland, which was not surprising given the portals the Fae liked to use, and he'd unapologetically used his magicks to quickly catapult himself to one of the top positions in a global food production company that produced everything from palm oil to polystyrene containers and plastic packaging. Profit was the name of the game, and Rian deliberately chose a company he knew cared more about the bottom line than they did for the environment. It was one way he could instantly stick it to the Earth Fae, though he was working on a longer plan for trying to seek specific revenge on those who had wronged him.

Namely, finding the man who was actually responsible for Rian's predicament.

In the meantime, he'd rake in his millions and live a lavish lifestyle, all while he counted the days until he could destroy the man who'd ruined him.

And then, maybe, just maybe, he'd finally find the peace he so desperately craved.

Seeing the redhead approach, Rian finished his fresh glass of whiskey. Though alcohol didn't have the same effect on him as it would humans, he could still get drunk if he committed himself to it — something which he did as regularly as he could.

"Keep the tab open. I'll settle up at the end of the month," Rian said.

"Aw, man, the night's still young," Cillian complained.

"It is at that. Have fun with it." Rian nodded and left, not caring what Cillian thought. It was one of the attributes that made him killer in the boardrooms. He said what he meant and did exactly what he wanted. And now? He wanted away from all of these people. The music was too loud, the walls were too close, and too many women sought his attention. It made his skin itch.

Ignoring the redhead who had dropped her tray and was pushing through the crowd to reach him, Rian turned down a hallway and ducked out a side exit, gulping the cool night air as fast as he'd just gulped his glass of whiskey. When the door shut behind him, it softened the noise from the club, as though he was hearing the sounds through water. Worry that the redhead would still seek him out danced through him, so he made his way down the dark alley, unconcerned for safety. There wasn't much that could hurt Rian, seeing as how his exile hadn't included a stripping of his powers. Perhaps it had been a mistake, or maybe they'd forgotten but, either way, with his knowledge of magicks, Rian was the only real threat in any dark alley in the city.

There was a bite to the air this evening, and Rian relished the slap of wind on his face when he turned the corner and followed the river toward his town house. Dublin was never a quiet city, but Rian liked her most like this, in the wee hours of the morning when traffic had slowed and stray bits of music from rowdy house parties drifted through the air. It was these times that he missed the wilds the most because, no matter how much he fought it, he was still an Earth Fae at heart. He'd always be more comfortable in nature than walking on concrete paths, but his life was no longer about what was most comfortable for him.

A song rose, one that had been niggling around his brain for months now, and he was just drunk enough to sing it softly in the quiet night. The words seemed to take on their own life, dancing from his lips and swirling beneath a beam of light from a streetlamp. He watched, bemused, as the tendrils of the song took to the air and disappeared into the night sky as though he was writing a love letter to the stars. He might as well have been, for it was his heartsong he was singing through the clutch that whiskey had on his rationality.

Unbidden, Terra's image rose to his mind.

He'd been thinking of her more of late, dreaming of her lush curves and the commanding tilt of her head. He hated her as much as he desired her, and his fingers dug into his palms as he walked, wishing to forget she ever existed. Terra was on his list for revenge, though he wasn't yet sure how he'd play it with her. First, he needed to find out who was responsible for his exile, then he'd work his way down his list.

And Terra, of pouty lips and bedroom eyes, would perhaps make an interesting companion before he ruined her. Yes, maybe that was the angle he'd take ... first he'd convince her to fall for him, and then he'd break her heart. It would be tricky, of course, if he was still in exile, but it would certainly be fun. Amused with his thoughts, Rian continued to hum his heartsong, no longer caring about the implications of sending his song out into the world, as it hardly mattered. No Fae could answer his heartsong if he was in exile.

Rian stumbled into his house, impatient with where his thoughts had gone, and slapped the switch for the lights. Instantly, he knew something was amiss. The energy of his home had shifted, a barely imperceptible disturbance in the force so to speak, and he held his hands in front of him as he scanned the room. A silvery glow emanated from his living room, and his heart sank.

Domnua.

It could only mean one thing — this night would end in battle. For while Rian didn't care for the Earth Fae, he certainly wasn't ready for the Domnua to take him down either. He'd fight until the end because, despite his unhappiness, he still valued his life.

"I see you, Dark Fae," Rian called, edging closer to his living room.

"I wanted you to see me." A sickly-sweet voice reached him, like strawberries gone sour, and Rian stepped into his sleek, modern living space to find the Goddess Domnu herself stretched across his sofa as though she owned the place. Behind her, several Domnua, their bodies silhouetted in a soft silvery glow, stood guard.

"The Goddess herself?" Rian laughed, rubbing a hand over his face. This night might turn out worse than he'd expected. Resigned, he met her eyes. "To what do I owe this displeasure?"

"You're a cheeky one, aren't you, Rian? But I like that about you. I've been watching you." Goddess Domnu stretched, her silver dress rippling across her body, her hair moving of its own accord. Upon closer inspection, Rian realized her hair was thickly coiled snakes, the ends nipping at the others as though they'd willingly eat each other.

"Is that right? See anything of particular interest to you?" Rian asked, raising his chin at her. He remained standing, waiting for her to speak. He felt like a mouse, waiting for a cat to pounce, and it was a feeling that didn't sit well with him. "If not, I'd really like to get some sleep."

"Oh yes." Goddess Domnu threw her head back and laughed, and Rian cringed when her hair laughed along with her. "I knew I'd like you. I'll get to the point, Rian, as it seems time is not on your side. I'm here to make a deal with you."

"A deal? That's unusual, isn't it? What could you possibly want with me? You're a goddess. Aren't you able to achieve anything you want with your level of power?"

"The true measure of power is knowing how, and when, to wield it. I require your services. In exchange, I'll grant you a reward of your choosing." The goddess crossed her arms over her voluptuous chest and pursed her lips. When the silence drew out, she arched a brow. "I'm surprised you're not jumping at this offer. Have I misread the situation? I was under the impression you wanted to destroy the Earth Fae for your exile."

"Ah, so it's the Earth Fae you're after." Rian was just drunk enough to lower himself into a chair across from

Domnu and steeple his fingers in front of him as he considered her words. "What do you want from them?"

"I want their amulet. With it, I can lead their people more easily. That's all."

"That's it? You want the knife, and I get what I want? Anything that I ask for?" Rian cocked his head, considering.

"You're still able to use their portal. Even in exile. Were you aware of that?"

At her words, Rian stilled.

"I was not aware of that," he bit out. "Are you certain? It was made clear that I was not to return." *He could have gone to his mother despite his exile.* Rage slid into his stomach, hot and sharp, and he stood to pace.

"You were ordered not to return. That does not mean you *can't* physically return."

"And if that's not the case? I'll die if I try to enter the portal." Rian pivoted, his mind whirling.

"You'll die either way. This is more of an order than a request, Earth Fae. You'll do well to take advantage of my generosity in this moment." Domnu's hair coiled around her face, the snake heads following Rian's movement.

"Terra wears the knife," Rian said.

"Then bring me Terra with the knife. Or kill her and bring the knife. I'm not picky."

"And in return?" Rian stopped in front of the goddess, trying not to show his distaste at her hair.

"What do you want most?" Domnu sent him a smoldering smile, and his head was filled with sultry thoughts of bodies writhing in the darkness. Rian shoved away the thoughts of sex that the goddess was projecting into his mind and focused on the one goal that had been his sole focus for years now.

"I want to find out which man is responsible for my exile, and I want him to pay."

"Are you sure?" Domnu trailed a finger across his thigh. Rian stepped back, breaking the contact, and watched storm clouds dance across the goddess's face. She was beautiful — in an 'eat your young' type of way — and Rian imagined lying with her would be both terrifying and intensely pleasurable. Until she bit his head off.

"Yes, I'm certain. I'll get the amulet for you, Goddess Domnu, so long as you deliver to me the man responsible for my exile."

"And it will be so."

Rian blinked at his now-empty living room, wondering briefly if he'd imagined the entire episode, and sank down into his chair. He stared out the window, where fog danced through a thin beam of light from a streetlamp and wondered if he'd just signed his own death sentence.

Did it matter though? He'd been dead inside for a long time now. Maybe, at least this way, he'd finally get answers. Now, he just had to work his magick to figure out how to sneak back through the portal and capture Terra.

The one woman he couldn't get out of his head.

3

THEIR HEARTSONG DRIFTED to her through the inky night, the words raining down on her like stars falling from the sky. Terra closed her eyes, feeling the brush of their song kiss her cheeks, and she drew a deep breath to calm herself.

This wasn't the first time that Rian had called to her, after all.

Did he realize what he was doing? Or who he was calling? Terra hurried to the stream, where she did all of her scrying, and pushed her worried thoughts aside to focus. It was a dumb twist of fate that had led her fated mate to be the same man who had torn her family apart. In theory, she needed to turn her back on Rian and focus on leading her people out of impending danger from the Dark Fae.

Which she could do, if she hadn't caught the look in Rian's eyes right before the door had closed on him, sentencing him to exile. Sure, there had been anger there, but it was the sadness and frustration that caught Terra's attention. It was the plea of an innocent man and, despite her family's protests, she'd spent time trying to uncover more information about the night Rian had been caught. The catastrophe that followed her investigation was enough to have her stop seeking answers, and she had left Eoghan to heal his partnership in peace.

The first time she'd heard her heartsong, Terra had been half-asleep, caught in a lucid dream where endless pleasure was bestowed upon her body by a blurry-faced man. She'd come fully awake, her hands on her body, gasping Rian's name as the song had trailed off into the early hours of dawn. She'd risen immediately, barely throwing a cloak over her body, before racing to the stream to try and conjure his image.

Much like she did now.

Terra pulled her dress over her head and stood in the soft light of the moon, ignoring the chill that the wind brought to her naked skin. There was something so peaceful and natural about going sky clad while she worked her magick. She crouched by the stream and whispered her spell, inviting the waters to show her Rian. The surface of the water shimmered, and Terra held her breath as she waited.

When no image appeared, she sat back on her haunches, considering what had gone wrong. Had she cast her spell wrong? It wasn't likely, as she was an expert at scrying, so what did this mean? Was Rian no longer in another realm?

"You should never wear clothes."

The voice, as intimate as a lover's, danced across her backside, sending a ripple of warning across Terra's skin.

Turning, she straightened, knife in hand, to find Rian leaning against a tree. Arms crossed, with his perpetual scowl across his darkly handsome face, Rian looked every inch the successful businessman.

And completely out of place in these woods.

Where had the man gone who used to practice his magicks barefoot among the trees, his hair rippling down his back in an unkempt manner? Now, everything about Rian was polished, from the tips of his shiny leather shoes to his carefully coiffed hair. A flash of gold at his wrist showcased a fancy watch that matched the gold at his belt. Terra studied him, searching for a glimpse of the man that she'd once ... well, she hadn't known him, really, but she'd always admired him from afar.

"My body is not for your commentary," Terra said, using her magick to wrap a layer of silk, inlaid with protective armor, around her body.

"It's a simple observation. Yours is a body made for touching. Strength and softness combined in one. Every day you wear clothes, you do a disservice to your beauty."

Terra pushed down the thrill his words brought to her, instead focusing on what was wrong with this situation. It was as though Rian was in the woods with her, but also not fully in the woods. She had an almost insatiable urge to stalk over to the tree and punch his stomach, just to see if he was real, of course.

"For everything I've learned about you, nothing indicated to me that you're hard of hearing. However, I'll reiterate ... my body is not yours to comment upon."

"It could be..." Rian arched an eyebrow and, despite herself, heat slid low into Terra's core.

"Why are you here?" Terra shifted the conversation.

"I don't know ... bored, I guess..." Rian shrugged a shoulder, looking around in pretended nonchalance. Terra hoped he was better at subterfuge in his business than he was in speaking to her, because it was clear he was lying.

"I'm finding that hard to believe. No need to dance around it, Rian. Why do you come to spy on me?" Terra kept her eyes on him, squinting as his form seemed to shift under the wan moonlight that filtered through the trees. Was he transporting the image of himself in some manner? He'd been legendary when it came to magicks, so she wouldn't be surprised if he'd worked out a way to travel here without fully being here.

"You know my name."

"Of course I do. And since we're commenting on bodies, why do I suspect yours is not here?" Terra stepped closer, squinting her eyes at his form.

"Ah, she of the wild woods and magick streams, unraveling my illusions so quickly." Rian blinked out of sight and, when he next spoke, it came from over her shoulder. Terra whirled, annoyed he'd gotten the edge on her.

"What do you want?" Terra asked, brandishing the knife in front of her. When his eyes dropped to the Earth Fae's amulet, her heart shivered. "No. Rian ... *no*. It's not yours to take."

"Just like it wasn't *my* punishment that I'm currently stuck with?" A sardonic grin crossed Rian's handsome face.

"Have you appealed your judgement?" Terra asked, stepping lightly back from his apparition.

"Have I..." Rian bit off the words and shook his head, anger clouding his features. "What's there to appeal, princess? I made my case, and everyone refused to believe me. You would know ... you were there."

"I've looked for more evidence since." Terra stilled when he stalked forward, until they stood barely a foot apart.

"I find that hard to believe. In fact, if I remember correctly, you were furious. If looks could kill and all that."

"Rian..." Terra gasped as the first wave of icy magick hit her gut, almost doubling her over, but her grip remained strong on the knife. This wouldn't be the first time that someone had tried to steal it from her, but it would certainly be one of her strongest adversaries. Hurriedly, she whispered an incantation, inviting the woods to take a stand. The trees behind her shifted, groaning as though the movement caused them to ache, and their branches swept down, knotting together in front of her to create a barrier between her and Rian.

"Do you think that will do much?" Rian laughed, and vanished, before appearing inside the makeshift branch cage with her.

"Yes, I do." Terra shifted, quickly running a spell that would force Rian to stay within the branches, rendering his power useless in this safe haven her Earth friends had created for her.

"Wait a minute..." Rian glanced down at his hands and then muttered under his breath, no doubt trying to run his own magicks on her. When nothing happened, Terra grinned.

"The Earth is our friend, Rian. Do you forget so easily?" Terra asked, keeping her hand tight around the hilt of her blade. The branches cocooned the two of them closely together, and she could pick out the flecks of gold in his moody green eyes.

"Like I was forgotten? Forsaken, even? Years of service to our people. And for what? To be exiled with little proof while my mother was on her deathbed." Rian's voice cracked, and Terra's heart twisted.

"And now? You seek revenge. To what purpose?" Terra was torn between wanting to hug her fated mate and throttle him. Did he even know they were mates? Had he sung their song on purpose?

"I'd rather die trying to destroy the Earth Fae than live knowing I've been exiled unfairly. My mother..." Rian shook his head. "Her last time seeing me was before a jury of our people convicting me. Can you imagine what that does to a mother? How she was shunned after? So yes, princess, I'll seek my revenge as I see fit. And it starts with that lovely knife of yours there."

Terra matched his stance, knowing she was protected in this woodland enclosure, and lifted her chin. His mother had warned Terra that Rian was a stubborn one. She'd spent time with Aster while trying to uncover the truth of the accusations against Rian and had learned something of the man's nature from his mother.

"You're working for the Domnua, aren't you? What did they promise you? You should know they rarely fulfill a promise. They'll use you and toss you aside."

"It won't be much different than my own people, will it then?" A wry smile crossed Rian's face before he vanished from sight. Terra took a moment, schooling her breathing, before turning and pressing a hand to the tree trunk in front of her. Her heart pounded in her chest, both from Rian's nearness, and from realizing how far he'd fallen.

"Thank you, brethren." Terra pressed her lips to the bark of the tree, and the branches behind her unknotted, freeing her from their protection.

Her path was now clear. Where once she thought that she could ignore Rian and save her people, now she knew it wasn't possible to separate the two. Rian had fallen into darkness and, with his life's mission to destroy the Earth Fae, if she left this loose end untethered, it could unravel her people.

Decided, Terra strode toward the castle to find Bianca and Seamus.

They were going to Ireland.

4

WHEN RIAN WOKE, his thoughts were already on Terra, obsessively reliving each moment she'd stood before him naked the night before. His body responded, and he fisted himself, stroking softly as he recalled every inch of her glorious curves in his mind.

She wasn't like the women he usually took to bed. Where his preferred type ran to skinny, with fake enhancements, there was nothing fake about Terra's rich curves. He hadn't been lying when he'd told her that hers was a body made for touching, and he'd clamped his hands tightly to resist reaching for her the night before. She was anything but skinny, instead she had muscular legs, a softly rounded stomach, and gorgeous breasts that begged for his attention. She was round, soft, and confident in a way that many people would kill for. Rian doubted that Terra ever thought about her weight as a detriment or something to fix, unlike the women he'd dated who constantly complained about bloating or hidden calories. Terra was the embodiment of an Earth

Goddess, deeply comfortable in her skin, and it made her all the more attractive to Rian.

Goddess, but he wanted her with every inch of his being. Rian groaned as he brought himself to completion, knowing whatever pleasure he took from the mere thought of Terra would be multiplied a million times over when he finally had his way with her. After the drink had worn off last night and he fully came to understand the agreement that he'd made, Rian had shifted his sights.

He still wanted to find the man who had ruined his life.

But first, he wanted Terra.

Her magicks were strong, as he'd expected, but even he had been surprised when she'd rendered his power ineffective so quickly the night before. Rian rose and strode naked to the shower, flipping on the steam jets to work at the kinks in his neck. Interest piqued, because it had been ages since anything had been a real challenge for him. And Terra? Not only would she be a worthy opponent, but he suspected she'd also be a delight in bed.

Rian groaned, resting his forehead against the shower wall, allowing the hot stream of water to pound his tense shoulders. Terra had been occupying his thoughts for months, and now he wondered if it had been some premonition that he would be tasked with capturing her for Goddess Domnu. Well, he didn't *have* to capture her. Domnu only cared about the knife that Terra carried and considered the woman dispensable. Which meant maybe there was a way that Rian could have both.

Killing Terra wasn't an option.

Rian had fallen, but he hadn't fallen that far. At least he hoped not. Maybe he was lying to himself about his reasons for not wanting to kill Terra and deliver the blade to Domnu, but if ever there was a time to lie to oneself it was in the comfort of one's shower in the soft light of morning. There was something about showers that let time be suspended for a moment, as though nothing and nobody could reach you, like a video game player hitting pause. Once he turned the water off and stepped out, real life would return. So in this quiet moment, Rian let the water soothe, as he worked hard to shore up his wall of anger at the Earth Fae and bury deep any admiration he had for the lushly beautiful Terra.

He had a job to do. One that required him to be focused, unattached, and ruthless.

Wrapping a towel around his waist, Rian strode to his closet, the lights flicking on when they sensed his movement. He pushed aside a row of custom suitcoats and keyed in a number next to a hidden door. When the lock beeped, Rian turned the knob and opened the door, light automatically illuminating the interior. It was a small space, just enough for him to step inside and walk three steps forward, but Rian hadn't needed much room to conceal the remnants of his former life. While he'd been exiled with only the clothes he'd been wearing at the time, Rian had spent a large chunk of his time since acquiring tools of Fae magicks. There was a black market for everything, Rian had quickly learned and with enough money at his disposal, he'd been able to acquire Fae items that had somehow fallen into human hands. He'd built his collection over the years and, while it didn't hold a candle to his original workroom back in the Fae realm, Rian had acquired enough tools to still be very dangerous.

Now, he studied the items placed carefully on the shelves, trailing a finger over wickedly sharp blades, silver potion bowls, and magicked arrows. He stopped when he came to the most dangerous item of all, the same iron cuffs that had been used to stifle his magick at the hearing, and he carefully wrapped those in a large magickal jeweler's cloth — which dulled the punch of pain from the iron. If he held his finger to the metal, his skin would blister and burn but, when wrapped, the iron merely felt hot to the touch. He'd use these to stun Terra, Rian decided, though his stomach twisted at the thought of marring that perfect skin of hers.

He'd have to think of a spell to dull the brute force of the cuffs on her delicate skin. Placing them into a leather satchel, Rian began to take his favorite tools from the closet, taking his time choosing what would be most advantageous to him on his quest. The bow and arrow was out, as it was clunky for travel, but three daggers of varying sizes, a sword, and a silver trapping net made it into the bag. For spells needing earth elements, Rian included his silver mixing bowl, several jars of charmed ingredients like saffron, rosemary, and crushed mollusk shells. A small quartz crystal, useful for channeling power, made it into the bag. Rian hefted the bag, gauging the weight and, satisfied that he was properly stocked while still being able to maneuver easily, he reached for his garments.

Simple fitted pants, similar to denim jeans that

humans wore, carried a protection spell woven into their threads. Very few blades would be able to pierce the cloth. Rian pulled an emerald-green long-sleeved shirt over his head, it melded to him like a second skin, and was infused with the same magick as his pants. The clothes weren't infallible against attack, but they were a helpful added layer of protection. Leather work boots with thick soles, and a grey knit hat completed the look, and Rian studied himself in the mirror in his main walk-in closet. The green of the shirt brought out the color of his eyes, and Rian leaned in, forcing himself to meet his own gaze. In his eyes, he found determination, but when he recognized another uncomfortable emotion, shame, he turned away. As far as he was concerned, he looked like any other lad going on holiday, and nothing about him would stand out to humans. Even his leather satchel, protected with magick, would look like a simple back-pack that students and hikers routinely carried.

"Cillian," Rian spoke into his phone as he grabbed his laptop and a thermos for coffee. "I'll be working remotely for a bit."

"Christ, Rian. It's barely seven in the morning. Where are you going?" A woman's voice murmured in the back-ground behind Cillian.

"It's no concern of yours." Rian had done a good job of keeping sharp boundaries with the people he worked with, and he leaned heavily on those now. "Send any business to my assistants. If anything major arises, I should be available."

Without waiting for a response, Rian clicked off the call and shoved the phone in his pocket. Business taken care of, as he'd emailed all three of his assistants about his plans, he picked up his bag and grabbed his car keys. It mattered little to him if the company suffered in his absence. He could just as easily rocket his way to the top of another business at any time he felt like it. Rian felt no loyalty to the company he worked for, and he was certain they felt none for him. In a profit-driven workspace, people were just numbers in a spreadsheet after all.

Rian unlocked his Land Cruiser and got in, knowing he could have transported himself to Grace's Cove if he'd really wanted to. However, he wanted the drive time to think about his tactics for capturing Terra, as well as not wanting to drain any of his energy for what was ahead. No, driving suited him just fine, and he flicked the radio off so he could be left in silence to think.

A part of him wished he hadn't gone to Terra after the Goddess Domnu had left him. It had been the whiskey driving his choices, as well as a deep-rooted need to see her. Now he feared he'd revealed too much about his intentions, as well as the depths of his magicks. Projecting himself into another place was a deeply difficult maneuver, and one not many Fae were capable of doing. If Terra hadn't been on alert prior to this, she was now. Rian cursed as he drummed his fingers on the steering wheel, annoyed with himself for his impulsiveness. He'd honed a reputation in the business world for being cold and calculating, and he'd need to draw on that experience if he was meant to fulfill his mission.

The drive passed quickly, with Rian barely registering the time, as he was so lost in thought. When he finally arrived at Grace's Cove, he pulled into a small parking lot by the harbor. Getting out, he stretched as he took in the small town. It was pretty, he'd give it that. Brightly colored buildings piled on top of each other along the harbor and rolling green hills hugged the town from behind. Empty slips showed the fishing boats were out for the day, and people strolled past on their way to the shops. It was charming, that was for sure, but still much too busy for what Rian had in mind. What he needed was isolation.

Spotting a bakery, Rian ducked in for a sausage roll to go, and wandered back to his car with the pastry in hand. He scrolled his phone, bringing up a map of the area, and studied the landscape. With the location of the portal in a fairly tricky and obscure spot, he'd need to move his captive quickly once he was back through. Could he deliver Terra to Domnu immediately? Sure. Was he going to? Not likely. Rian couldn't quite understand it, but he needed more time with her.

Rian narrowed his eyes at the Blasket Islands on the map and considered the possibilities. He took a screenshot and sent the info to his assistant with the instructions to secure lodging — no matter the price. If she was as expedient as she usually was, he'd have a place to stay by the end of the day. In the meantime, Rian decided to go scope out the location of the portal and see if he could sense any wards or other Fae magicks in the area.

The portal was once located on a remote beach, sheltered by high cliff walls. If it was still there, Rian would need to bring Terra through and immediately transport her to one of the Blasket Islands, which wasn't all that far.

Location wise, his decision to bring Terra through alive and question her made sense.

Had she really looked for evidence to help him?

The thought sprung unbidden to his mind as he parked his car near a small stone cottage and crossed a gently sloping field to the edge of the cliff that jutted proudly into the air. Far below him, waves lapped at a pretty sand beach, and the air brought a taste of the sea with it. Closing his eyes, he shoved thoughts of Terra aside and focused on his magick, locating the pulse of the portal easily. Still, it stood, and it was a wonder that no Domnua had destroyed the doorway to the Fae realm yet.

Which meant they found it useful.

"No blood shall be spilled on my land, Fae."

Turning, Rian took in the woman behind him. Dressed for yard work in dirty jeans and a work shirt, strawberry blonde hair tumbled over her shoulders and whiskey brown eyes regarded him warily. Interesting. There was a hint of otherness to this woman, but Fae she was not. A dog sat at her side, cocking its head at him, and he barely stopped himself from smiling at the animal. He'd always had a weakness for dogs.

"Is it your land then? Do you own the sea as well?" Rian asked, lifting his chin and shooting her a cocky grin which only served to deepen the scowl on her face.

"I might, at that. Are you willing to find out then?" The woman crossed her arms over her chest, her eyes shooting daggers, and Rian found himself warming to her. He'd always admired strong women.

"How do you know I'm Fae?" Rian avoided her

comment about blood being spilled. He wasn't in the habit of making promises he couldn't keep.

"The lot of you are easy enough to spot, and that's the truth of it. What with your glow and all." The woman waved a hand in the air, and amusement filled Rian. His glow?

"Is that right? You're the first I've met who sees this glow. Dare I say that you're not of this world either?" Rian rocked back on his heels as he studied her.

"Oh, I'm more of this world than yourself. You'll not be troubling yourself with my lineage unless you cross me. On you go then. I've plans for my day, and they don't include mopping up Fae blood."

"You're so certain it would be my blood?" Rian arched an eyebrow.

"Is that a threat?"

Rian turned as the ocean roared behind him, and he was shocked to see the once peaceful water now roiling with vicious waves. Dark clouds thundered across the horizon, and Rian's admiration grew. One who could summon the weather was certainly a friend of the Fae.

"Not today. I'll just be on my way then." Rian held up his hands as though he was acknowledging defeat. It wouldn't do him any good to pick a fight with this woman, whatever she was, when he'd already obtained the information he needed. Giving her a mocking bow, he turned and strolled toward his car.

When his heartsong rippled across the water, the sea breezes delivering it to him with a kiss, Rian skidded to a halt. Whirling, he discovered the meadow behind him empty. Did this woman know his fated mate? Never had he heard it sung, and now his heart split in two, aching for a love that he could never know.

Biting his lip, Rian closed his eyes and mentally imagined frost forming around his heart until the promise of new love was frozen over by a thick layer of ice. There, that was better. With no emotions to speak of, Rian would be free to continue on his task for the Domnua.

Turning, he strode across the field and never looked back.

5

"WHY DO YOU SING HIS HEARTSONG?" Bianca asked, the pretty blonde stuffing her pack for their journey.

"I never have before. I'm hoping to confuse him, maybe break through to him a bit, and to lure him closer. It's powerful magick, our heartsong, and he should be helpless to resist it," Terra explained.

When she'd returned to the castle, Terra had met with Callum, Lily, Bianca, and Seamus. Callum had agreed to lend her the support of Bianca and Seamus, but the other Elemental Fae leaders needed to stick close. Now that they were aware that the Domnua were infiltrating their villages, high level power was needed to protect against the Dark Fae.

"And you're hoping to use your feminine wiles to bed him and convince him to abandon his plan to steal the amulet?" Bianca surprised Terra by holding her hand out for a high five. Bewildered, Terra tapped her palm.

"Um, I'm not sure I would have looked at it exactly like that?" Terra crinkled her brow.

"Whoops, sorry. Is that disrespectful to your heart-song and all? Saying that you'll use hot sex to stun the enemy into submission?" Bianca's bright blue eyes were hopeful and, despite herself, Terra chuckled.

"I suppose it could be a weapon of choice if need be," Terra said. She didn't like the thought of using a fated mate bond for ulterior motives, but these weren't normal times.

"Men have used it against women for centuries. No reason not to flip the script," Bianca mused, her face lighting up when Seamus entered the room.

"That's me all set," Seamus said, dropping a kiss on Bianca's lips. A flutter of something ... not jealousy, more like longing, moved through Terra. Though she was well used to being on her own, often preferring it, there was something about the easy confidence of a well-balanced union between two people who clearly adored each other that made her reconsider the benefits of having a partner. Granted, she suspected that a union between her and Rian would be anything but easy, but that wasn't for her to decide.

The Fates had their whims.

"Did you want to have a team meeting before we go?" Bianca asked, closing her pack and putting it on the table in front of them. They had met in an interior lounge room of one of the apartments in the castle, and a fire crackled merrily in the hearth, while soft music played in the background. Rich velvet tapestries hung on the marble walls, and soft furniture meant for lounging and other activities was scattered through the large room.

"A team meeting?" Terra crinkled her brow, marveling

at the words. The word team was not really used often in her world.

"You know, to just talk about our goals and how we plan to achieve them? An action plan?"

"My love does so enjoy action plans. If I show her a neatly written to-do list, it's like foreplay," Seamus said, grinning down at Bianca.

"He's not wrong." Bianca sighed and clapped her hands in front of her chest. "So tell us ... how can we serve?"

"Have you been briefed on Rian?" Terra asked, turning from where she was double-checking her pack to make sure she had her treasured magicks with her. The dagger remained strapped to her leg, though she'd moved it higher to her thigh. A slit cut in the pocket of her dress allowed her easy access to the blade if needed.

"Just that he's your fated mate and he's been exiled," Seamus said, scratching his shock of red hair. The man was like a lanky sapling, Terra mused, and she suspected his strength was likely often underestimated.

"Rian was once head of magicks training for the Earth Fae. Which means he's incredibly powerful, highly skilled, and likely knows more about magicks than he was ever allowed to teach. On top of that, he's always claimed his innocence, and his mother died while he's been exiled. If his story is true, and he is innocent, his motive to harm the Earth Fae is a strong one. It's not entirely a surprise that the Domnua have found their way to him and likely convinced him to act against us. I don't know that he would make a play for our amulet unless they were involved, though I can't be certain. The events of late certainly make it seem so. I think, to be safe, we'll need to assume the Domnua are involved. Which means, at all times, we'll need to be on watch for the Dark Fae to make a move."

"And we'll be facing off with a master of magick who has a strong vendetta against the Earth Fae. Got it." Bianca nodded vigorously. "What's the plan then?"

"I don't have a great one, sure it's sad for me to admit that." Terra sighed. "There's not much that can be done in the way of capturing Rian or disarming his magick until we're actually with him."

"First stop. Find Rian." Bianca held a finger up.

"After we find him, we either convince him to change his mind, disable him, or capture him." Terra winced, thinking about having to harm Rian.

Though she'd put on a careless face the night before, his leisurely study of her naked body and his wide-eyed appreciation of her assets had left her aching for his touch. She supposed that must be the way of things with fated mates that, no matter the situation, their attraction would always be strong. She'd have to fight her pull to him, knowing he'd use his power on her, and instead stay focused on what was best for her people. It certainly put her in a precarious position but, at the end of the day, Terra was only one woman. She believed in the good the Earth Fae did for the environment and the world. If she had to sacrifice her chance at a happy future in order to save her people, well, she'd do so in a blink of an eye.

"Let's start with the lowest form of that, shall we?" Bianca said, an empathetic look on her pretty face.

"Maybe we'll have a wee chat and a cuppa tea and be home for dinner."

"Ah, my love. Ever the optimist." Seamus laughed. He nodded to their bags. "Shall we get on with it then? To the portal?"

"Yes, to the portal. I've sung our heartsong for the first time ever, which should hopefully have the effect of drawing Rian close to the portal. If not, I'll sing it once more upon arrival. It's not likely he'll be able to resist, no matter how many magickal tricks he employs, so we'll know when he is near. Once he's close — be prepared. We have no idea if he'll attack immediately, and I would deeply prefer neither of you to come to harm."

"We've weathered our fair share of battles now, haven't we?" Bianca winked at Seamus and then turned back. "*It's also foreplay*," she mouthed to Terra.

Terra bit back a grin and slipped the strap of her satchel over her shoulder. Touching the gold circlet of leaves at her head, she closed her eyes for a moment to center herself. In her head, she imagined being in the circle of trees by her favorite stream, her bare feet connecting to the Earth. The power of her people and the natural world hummed in her blood, and her purpose was pure. Opening her eyes, she looked at the two who were putting their lives on the line to help her.

"Thank you for being willing to accompany me. I want to caution you that portal travel can be disorienting and, once through, it may take a few moments to gather your wits."

"Yes, it is a bit dizzying, isn't it?" Bianca said, following Terra as they left the lounge through a narrow hallway that descended several flights of stairs until it deposited them into a side courtyard. There, two guards waited for them, their heavy gold armor at odds with the Flower Fae who flitted among the rose bushes planted along the stone walls. The guards would guide them to the portal entrance, concealing their path from all Fae, as secrecy was vital when it came to the location of the portals. There was more than one, and even Terra didn't know the location of all of the gateways but, as a leader, she did have knowledge of a few.

"Can you imagine the cost of a suit of armor made of gold?" Bianca gawked at the guards, stopping just short of running her hand over their suits. Seamus caught her hand in time and tucked it by his side, a grin on his face. When he smiled, Seamus went from gawky to starkly handsome, and Terra was beginning to understand why Bianca was so attached to him. That and his undying adoration of her.

"Best not to touch, doll," Seamus said.

"Oh right. That's rude of me, isn't it then? Could you imagine if a stranger came up and stroked my shirt?" Bianca laughed at herself, and Terra was grateful for their easy chatter. Though she was one to prefer the sounds of nature, too much silence allowed her thoughts to turn down dark paths. The light conversation between Bianca and Seamus served as just enough distraction to break the tension that weighed heavily on her shoulders, while also managing not to be an annoyance.

After a thirty-minute walk that led across a field, through a sliver of Terra's beloved forest, and down a rocky slope to the water, the guards turned to Terra.

"We've arrived." Both guards bowed their heads respectfully.

"Thank you for your escort." Terra approached the narrow crack in the rock wall and ran her hands over the sun-warmed rocks. No dark magick burned her palms, so she turned back with a brisk nod to the others. "Onward."

"I swear, these crevices get narrower and narrower, don't they?" Bianca griped, and Terra smiled. No, the passageway was not suited for a large woman such as herself, but she knew enough about the mercurial magick of the Fae to know that looks were deceiving. It was likely simply an illusion to discourage any passerby from attempting to navigate the crevice, if anyone even got that far. There would be enough wards charmed with magick to repel even the most curious of Fae. Pressing forward, she slipped easily through the entrance.

"Ohhhh," Bianca whispered after her, catching on to the magick at play. "Cool."

In only a few moments, the passageway led them to a small cavern where a fire crackled in the corner.

"Damn it. Do we have to jump through fire again? I hate this part," Bianca moaned to Seamus. "I know it won't hurt me, but years of conditioning make me think otherwise."

"That's what it's meant to do," Terra said.

"I get it. I do. It's just ... not a favorite," Bianca sighed. They gathered in a small half circle around the fire. Terra slipped a dagger from its holster at her side. She wouldn't use the Earth Fae's dagger when going through a portal, just in case she lost her grasp of it in the uncertain moments after their arrival, but she still wanted to be prepared for any threat on the other side.

"Arm yourselves. We'll go as one." Terra waited until the others had similar blades in their hands.

"As fire burns to ashes and returns to earth whence it was born, we now travel through, our pure purpose sworn," Terra murmured and together the three stepped into the fire. For a moment, everything went black, and Terra felt as though she was disconnected from her body, an untethered soul, drifting blissfully in nothingness. The return was a jarring one, and Terra gasped for air as they tumbled from the fire into another cavern.

A rope slipped around her neck, and though Terra sliced upwards with her blade, her weapon was knocked easily from her hand. She blinked, trying to shake the cloudiness from her brain, calling upon the power that coursed deeply inside of her.

Cold metal clasped her wrists, their immediate sting causing her shoulders to crumple in defeat. Iron cuffs. She didn't have to look up to know that Rian had been waiting for them to arrive.

"Terra!" Bianca shouted, but a wave of magick pulsed across the room, stunning her still dizzy companions. Though Seamus launched an attack, Rian quickly disarmed the both of them, binding the two together with what Terra assumed was a charmed rope. Worry slipped through her. She'd known an attack was a possibility, but she'd expected it from the Domnua which were easier to fight as they operated on brute force and sheer stupidity. But Rian? He'd planned for their arrival. She'd miscalculated by assuming he wouldn't know where the portal was.

This was her fault, and she winced as she struggled against the cuffs that burned into the delicate skin at her wrists.

"Lovely of you all to join me," Rian said. He rocked back on his heels and clapped his hands together. "I've been waiting for you. Best to hurry on. I can't be sure how many more of you are along for your trip."

With that, Rian hooked his arms around all three of them, and though Seamus tried to head butt him, Rian easily avoided harm. When a sucking sensation pulled at Terra's legs she understood what Rian was doing.

They were being transported somewhere, and it wasn't likely she was going to be happy about it. Anger simmered low in her stomach, and she raised her head to meet Rian's gaze. His face was inches from hers, and she was tempted to bite his nose, she was so angry with him. Didn't he have any clue that he was fighting for the wrong side? Amusement danced in his moody green eyes, and he shifted his head back as though he understood her thoughts.

"Shame," Terra whispered.

"It's a good thing that I stopped feeling emotions a long time ago, isn't it?" Rian said. "Now, let me be the first to welcome you to your new home."

6

"SIR," Callahan, Rian's butler, bowed his head as though Rian was a king arriving with esteemed guests. "Welcome to Inis na Bró. I hope our guests will be comfortable here."

Rian had found Callahan on one of his nightly walks through the dark streets of Dublin. The two had instantly recognized each other as Elemental Fae, though Callahan was of the Fire Fae, and Rian had given the older man a job. While Callahan wasn't exiled from the Fae realm, he'd left long ago, never feeling like he much fit in the Fae world, and now he happily saw to managing Rian's life. If Rian decided to thaw any of the ice around his heart, he might even say that Callahan had taken to filling a father's role in his life, but he preferred not to think too deeply about that. For his part, Callahan acted as moral compass of sorts for Rian, doing his best to not let him fall too deeply into the darkness, and he'd had more than a few choice words for Rian when he'd learned of his agreement with the Domnua.

Rian suspected loyalty was one of the only reasons Callahan had even agreed to come here today. That, and likely his desire to protect Rian's captives. It was a fine line Rian was walking, and Callahan reminded him of that when worry slipped into his eyes at the cuffs on Terra's wrists.

"Have accommodations been sorted out?" Rian asked, ignoring the disapproval in Callahan's eyes.

"Yes, sir. It's astonishing what an obscene amount of money, coupled with a touch of Fae magick can accomplish in a short amount of time." Callahan tugged on the newsboy cap that he wore over his thatch of white hair. A tweed waistcoat with a watch chain added to the impression that he could be anyone's kindly grandfather. Rian understood more than anyone how looks could be an illusion.

"That's grand. Thank you for that," Rian said. Turning, he addressed his three captives who stared mutinously at him. The brain fog from traveling through the portal had worn off quickly, and now angry energy crackled around the three of them. Rian knew the instant he removed their bindings that they would make a move on him. "Let's just get this out of the way, shall we? I'm not interested in harming any of you. The island has been set with protective wards, and you will be unable to transport from its borders. I would like to take your bindings off, particularly Terra's, because while I did my best to magick the cuffs so they wouldn't burn her skin too much, they'll still be hurting her. Will you give me your word that you won't try to attack me or, more importantly, Callahan?"

"What would our word mean to someone like you?" Seamus spit at Rian's feet.

Rian took a moment, looking from the ground and then back to Seamus as he schooled his impatience.

"I don't lie. I don't cheat. And I always keep my word." Rian held Seamus's eyes.

"And your word is that we won't come to harm here?" Terra asked, drawing his attention away from Seamus. Rian didn't like where his thoughts went when he looked at her. It was as though she could see into what was left of his soul, as though she still had hope for him. Her careful assessment made him want to squirm, a reaction that he decidedly did not like.

"My word is that I won't bring you harm. Nor will Callahan. I can't promise beyond that. I don't like to speak for anyone else." Rian tore his gaze away from the curvy beauty, his hands itching to touch her, and looked across the island. Rolling green hills led to jagged cliffs, a stark contrast to the soft meadow behind him, and Rian recalled those cliffs being referred to as a cathedral of sorts. Sharp rocks jutted in pillars from the ocean, forming almost an arch, and acted as a deterrent for anyone wishing to access the island from the sea.

"So why bring us here?" The blonde spoke, drawing his attention back. He hadn't caught her name yet. "Are you wanting to form an alliance? Make friends? Keep us out of harm's way? What's your goal?"

Her questions annoyed him, largely because he didn't have an answer for them. What he should have done was deliver Terra quickly to the Domnua and satisfy his end of the agreement. He turned away.

"Callahan will see to you." Rian strode away, but not before he heard Callahan murmuring an apology to Terra for the marks on her wrists, and it took everything in his power not to return to her and see for himself the damage he'd wrought on her delicate skin. The thought of hurting her didn't sit well with him, which was a thought he'd have to examine more deeply at another time. Rian wasn't prone to fits of introspection, and he didn't like where his thoughts were going now that he had launched this haphazard plan of his. What he needed to keep his focus on was his end goal — retribution for the wrongs against him.

Rian was only keeping Terra because he wanted to know if she'd really tried to find out more about the man responsible for his exile. If so, maybe, just maybe, she'd be an ally in his cause to overturn his judgement. She was the key to answers for him — not Domnu. It wasn't likely the Dark Goddess would actually deliver the man responsible for his exile. *That* was his reason for keeping Terra close. Having resolved the issue in his mind, he continued his trek toward the cliffs. It wasn't like he had any idea where he was going, he just needed to put distance between himself and the others.

For years now, Rian's single-minded focus had directed every thought and action that he made. But seeing the way Terra looked at him had thrown his usually swift decision-making process into turmoil. Rian didn't like being out of control, and he needed to center himself before he returned to deal with his captives.

Rian paused at the edge of the cliffs, staring down at the cathedral rocks. An angry sea crashed into the base of the rocks, the waves splintering and turning over on themselves, and Rian caught a glimpse of a Water Fae flitting through the water. He wasn't surprised they'd found him already, though there wasn't much they could do. The other benefit of no longer being in service to the royal court? He'd had a lot of time to study and strengthen his magick. It would take an exceptionally powerful Fae to break the spells he'd placed around this island. He went back to studying the pillars of rocks, his eyes caught on how proudly they jutted into the sky, ignoring the ocean that threatened to drag them down.

Humans may see a cathedral, a place of worship, but all Rian saw was a reminder that stubbornness equaled perseverance.

"I've locked their rooms, as requested."

Rian didn't turn at Callahan's disapproving tone, instead watching several gulls swoop and dive between the narrow pillars of rock. It looked like great fun, to be able to dip and turn in such a precarious manner, gliding through the air.

Rian couldn't remember the last time he'd had fun.

"Thank you," Rian said, and paused before adding, "Is ... Terra unharmed?"

"Her wrists have burns, and she could scar. I was under the impression you'd protected the cuffs?" Callahan sniffed, and Rian glanced over to see the man regarding him with a disapproving look.

"I did. You know as well as I do that iron is a difficult metal for us."

"Well, she's in great pain. And you've done this to her, so I hope you can make amends. Particularly since you said you wouldn't harm them. How are they supposed to believe your word when you've already broken your promise?" Callahan's words stung, like icy flecks of water from the angry sea below, and Rian turned on his heel.

"Show me where they are."

"She's a lovely woman, you know," Callahan commented, easily keeping pace with Rian as they crossed the uneven terrain.

"I wouldn't, actually." Rian didn't need the old man getting any matchmaking ideas. He'd been trying for ages to get Rian to abandon his plan of revenge and to settle down with a sweet girl. Every time Rian pointed out that Callahan had failed to do the same, the old man had just laughed it off claiming he'd already enjoyed the love of his lifetime and that was enough to keep his heart warm forever. A sentiment that Rian didn't rightly understand, or care to know, but *he'd* never pushed a woman on Callahan. Yet the man refused to acknowledge Rian's requests that he stop trying to find him a woman.

"She has kindness. Not all people do, but it radiates from her. But don't let her softness fool you either, boyo. There's great power that lies within her. You'd do well to respect that."

"Who says I don't?" They crested a hill, and Rian paused at the top, marveling at the view before him. Somehow Callahan had managed to transform abandoned ruins into abundant accommodations for them. The stone walls that still stood from the old settlement had been incorporated into the new, and the result was like one of those high-end glamping experiences posh people preferred over roughing it in the wilds. Canvas roofs, wood pillars, and elevated floors would keep occupants dry and off the ground, and streams of smoke poured merrily from metal chimney pipes. Two of the cottages had doors that were closed, and Rian assumed those were where his captives were being kept.

"Terra is in the cottage to the left. Your accommodations are..." Callahan trailed off as Rian strode toward Terra's cottage, dismissing the man. With a flick of his hand, Rian unlocked the magick that held the door closed and pushed into the one-room cottage. There, he found Terra sitting on the edge of a bed, stroking her wrists, head bent. Something unfamiliar squirmed in his gut, a long-forgotten emotion, and Rian ignored it as Terra shot to standing.

"Let me see your wrists." Rian held out his hands, his tone brooking no argument, and Terra held out her hands.

"It's fine," Terra began, but stopped speaking when Rian leveled an angry look at her.

It wasn't fine. Not in the slightest. His breath hissed out when he saw the red welts marring her delicate skin, and he cradled her wrists gently as he tamped down at the anger that threatened to boil over. Not anger at her, of course, but himself. It was the one emotion he rarely blocked, because anger was the fuel that kept his vision for revenge alive. Now, though, he admonished himself for not doing a better job with magicking the iron cuffs that had bound Terra's wrists.

"It's not fine. I promised you that you wouldn't come to harm at my hands." Terra's skin heated beneath his fingers and, despite his concern for her wounds, Rian couldn't help but flash back to seeing her naked body in all its impossible beauty when he'd visited her by the stream. The desire to touch almost overwhelmed him, and he found himself stroking the insides of her wrists with the lightest of touches. When she trembled at his touch, he stopped, his eyes spearing hers. "I'm sorry. I'm hurting you."

"No..." Terra whispered, her pupils dilating, her voice breathy. "You're not ... it's not..."

Rian knew that look on a woman, but he hadn't expected to see it on Terra's face. Not for him, that is. The ice cracked, and his anger poured through, heating and morphing to lust, and he did what he'd been aching to do for months now when he'd dreamt of her.

Rian kissed her, frustration making him more forceful than necessary, and heat speared him as she gasped against his lips. Dropping her wrists, he dove his hands into her hair and angled her head, wanting, no ... *needing*, more of her. She tasted of honey and something effervescent ... like moonlight dancing across a fairy garden, and he savored her kiss as though it was the most precious of sweets. When she moaned, stumbling slightly against him, Rian broke the kiss and wrapped his arms around her, pulling her close for a moment. They stood like that, breathing in tune to each other, and Rian bent his forehead to hers. He had no idea what he was going to do with this intoxicating woman.

Her scent teased him, and he shifted, trailing his lips to her neck, determined to imprint her on his mind. There was the honey again, but also something earthy and fresh, like diving into a frigid mountain stream. He inhaled deeply, as though he could take this piece of her with him, and he pressed a kiss to the soft spot behind her ear. Rian eased his arms from around her, and found her wrists once more, though he kept his face buried at her neck. With each breath, Terra's body trembled beneath his, and he couldn't help but wonder — was it fear or lust?

Working quickly, before he did something stupid like drop to his knees and bury his head between her legs to worship at the altar of the most beautiful woman he'd ever seen, Rian pulled at his thread of magick and poured it into his hands that circled Terra's wrists.

"Oh, Rian," Terra gasped out, turning her head slightly so that her lips were close to his. "You've taken the pain. You didn't have to do that. I would have been able to heal myself, I'm sure."

"As I said ... you'll not come to harm at my hands." She'd come to pleasure though, if he had any say about it. Rian had no idea what had transpired to take him from merely lusting after this woman to desiring her so strongly that he was certain he'd kill for her, but the one thing he now understood was that he had to have Terra. Already he was calculating ways to protect her from the Domnua.

The idea of someone having this type of power over him didn't sit well with Rian. He needed to get his head back in the game and put his walls back up. Try as he might, he was currently struggling with keeping the wall up around his emotions.

This was all Callahan's fault, Rian decided, as he dropped Terra's wrists and took two large steps backwards. A ray of sunlight speared through the window, catching the glinting gold tones in her warm hair. Her mouth hung slightly open, faintly pink from his kiss, and her eyes widened as she watched him retreat. If ever a woman looked appetizing enough to bed, it was this one.

Swearing, Rian stormed from the cottage and threw a furious glance at a grinning Callahan.

"Stay out of it, old man."

"Me? I'd never meddle, and that's the truth of it." Callahan's cheery whistle was all Rian needed to hear, and he swore once more.

Just what had he gotten himself into?

7

TERRA PACED HER COTTAGE, unused to being stuck inside, and relived every moment of their kiss. The intensity of emotion had sent desire coursing through her body, and she was certain Rian was equally as touched as she had been. Which made her wonder — did he know they were fated mates? While one of her magickal abilities allowed her to see what others couldn't, through scrying, that didn't mean that Rian had the same.

A knock sounded at the door, and Terra whirled as a cool breeze with the taste of the sea entered along with Callahan. He held a tray of food and was followed by Bianca.

"Refreshments for you ladies. Miss Bianca wished to speak with you." Callahan's gaze darted to Terra's wrists where Rian had erased her wounds. "Ah, I see Rian has attended to you. Do you still have any pain?"

Just in my heart.

"No, thank you, Callahan," Terra said instead.

"If you need anything, just knock on the door, and I'll be here to help."

"What we need is the freedom to walk around. If Rian says we can't transport from the island, what's the point in keeping us locked up?" Bianca demanded, hands on her hips.

"I'll take it up with him." Callahan ducked his head through the low doorframe and shut the door quietly behind him.

"I like him," Terra said, dropping onto one of the benches next to the small table where Callahan had placed a tray of food. "I feel like he's on our side."

"Did you catch how disappointed he seemed in Rian? There's definitely something amiss there. The evil overlord usually has evil henchmen, and I'm not getting that vibe from Callahan either," Bianca agreed. She sat as well and picked up the pot of tea. "Tea?"

"Please."

"So, give me all the details. I see Rian healed you. What's that about?" Bianca picked up a biscuit from the tray and nibbled on it as she eyed Terra's healed wrists.

"He ... it was like he was a different man. As soon as he saw the marks on my wrists, he turned all angry and protective." Terra touched her lips, and Bianca perked up.

"This sounds promising ... go on," Bianca encouraged.

"He kissed me."

"Yes!" Bianca fist pumped the air. "The man does have a heart."

"A well-guarded one at that." Terra took a biscuit from the tray and nibbled on it absentmindedly while she tried to puzzle out what to do about Rian. "He seemed angrier about the kiss than pleased, though it lit me up all the way down to my toes. He was upset with himself that his magick hadn't been enough to protect me from the iron cuffs."

"So he's protective of you... That's not a bad thing. It's confusing, isn't it? What he's doing with us here?" Bianca tapped a finger to her lips as she thought about it. "I can't help but think it's because of you. Otherwise, wouldn't he have just stolen the dagger off of you while you were cuffed and called it a day?"

"I did note that we weren't disarmed when we were put in our rooms." The amulet was still strapped to her thigh, gently pulsing with power, a constant reminder of just who she was and the people that she represented. It would do her well to remember who she stood for and temper any impulsive choices she may have when she was around Rian. Until she could understand the game he was playing, her safest bet was to err on the side of being a leader and to continue to stand for her people.

"That's also strange. Like ... you could have stabbed him when he was kissing you, and we'd be on our way, right?" Bianca mused. Terra winced at the thought of stabbing her fated mate. It wouldn't be an ideal position, no, but she'd do it if she had no choice. She hoped their circumstances wouldn't bring her to having to make such a difficult decision. Hers was but one life, Terra reminded herself. Her people were of the thousands. Not to mention the generations to come. No, it wouldn't do to be selfish. Matters of the heart often faded in the background of war.

"I sense some confusion from him."

"You know what we need to do?" Bianca snapped her fingers, bouncing on the bench so that the teacups rattled on the table. Terra grabbed hers before tea could slosh over the edge.

"What's that?"

"We need to make him fall in love with you." Bianca beamed at her like she'd solved all their problems.

"You say it like it would be so easy." Terra laughed at Bianca's excited expression.

"It *would* be though. Listen ... there are a lot of unanswered questions about Rian, right? And he's just ... well, I think he must be fighting some sort of internal battle here. Based on what you told me about being exiled when his mother died, and how he's claimed his innocence, I'm guessing he's just really, really angry. Maybe he's locked down his emotions, maybe he's focused on revenge for so long, and that's all he knows. But!" Bianca held a finger in the air. "That doesn't mean that a fair maiden can't come along and be a ray of sunshine that pierces the darkness of his stormy soul. That's where you come in. *You're* the ray of sunshine. We just need to wear him down until he has no choice but to fall in love with the awesomeness of you. I mean ... just look at yourself. It shouldn't be all that hard to do. I give it a week, tops."

Terra laughed, amused by Bianca's enthusiasm.

"Thank you for the compliment, my friend, but I don't think it is possible to force anyone to love me."

"Maybe not, but we have a winning card, don't we? We already know he's your fated mate. Doesn't that mean he'll automatically have an affinity for you? Like you're catnip, and he's a cat who can't resist?"

"Um..." Terra wasn't sure what catnip was, but she could grasp the meaning. Sometimes Bianca's human-world references confused her. "While a fated mate connection will make the feelings more powerful, it's not always destined to be. Both mates must also choose to claim the other."

"That's right. Can you just claim him then?"

"It's a touch more involved than that. You don't just go up to him and declare him yours. He's not a plaything," Terra said.

"I mean, he *could* be a plaything."

Terra remembered how his lips had felt on hers, and the way his kiss had illuminated her insides like the first kiss of sun in the early dawn.

"I do think your idea has merit. Unlike men, who tend to come to war and battle with brute force, perhaps figuring out how we can get Rian to align with us will better serve our people."

"Listen to you," Bianca gushed. "You sound so regal. But ... doesn't that feel a little bit yucky? When you phrase it that way? My thoughts aren't about forming an alliance with Rian. That sounds so ... clinical. What I mean is that, since you're already on the path to love, why not help it along?"

"I'm not on the path to..." Terra trailed off as her heart warmed in her chest when she thought about Rian's kiss once again. Right, so perhaps it had meant more to her than she'd realized. "Hmm. Maybe I am? It's hard to say..."

"You don't have to have all the answers right now. I do think if he is already your fated mate, why not nudge him along on the path toward discovering his love for you? In that way, you can hopefully fall for each other and become a united front in helping the Earth Fae. I don't see it as a tool of battle, so much as a circumstance that could be used to benefit a greater cause."

"It's worth a try." Terra worried that her heart would hurt, dearly, if he rejected her, but at least she'd be able to say she'd tried. "What's your plan?"

"Okay, I think this is going to be fun. Well, as much as we can have while we're stuck here. Let's think about this. What are some of the basic things that men fall for all the time?" Bianca grabbed another biscuit and munched on it as she thought.

"Being naked usually works," Terra offered.

"Ah yes, the most basic of male attention grabs," Bianca said. "Effective, but we might need something more subtle to start. What else?"

"I think he needs someone to care for him. He's been shoved out of our society and left alone. I can imagine that's, well, lonely."

"Excellent observation. He's lonely, angry, and you say he claims he's innocent. Do you believe him to be?"

"In some respects, I don't actually want to believe him." Terra plopped her head on her hands on the table. "But I might have to."

"Why don't you want to believe him?"

"Because then I have to find out who actually cheated with my brother's fated mate. And who *actually* has caused so much pain for my family. I tried gathering more information, I really did. But I was just met with so much resistance, and his wife refuses to speak of it. My brother was so grateful to have answers, and though his relationship with his wife still struggles, it's much better now."

"I didn't know it was your brother." Bianca's mouth dropped open. "No wonder this is tricky for you. What else did you find out? Also, why is cheating a crime for your people?"

"Cheating isn't a crime necessarily. Cheating with a royal fated mate? One who has a claimed bond? That's a crime. I understand it doesn't make sense, but it's really important for the Fae to uphold the sanctity of the bond. Once a fated mate couple claims each other, their magick doubles, if not triples, in power. Because of that, we've had instances where Fae have tried to fake claims or arranged fated unions in order to gain more magick. It never works, as the Fates always find a way of dealing with imposters, but the Fae are particularly severe in this respect."

"And here I thought the Fae were all ... party all night and free love with everyone. I swear, it felt like Woodstock or something the night of the celebration for the Queen's life."

"Oh, we absolutely believe in free and natural love with all. It's a Fae's right to choose. See, if a Fae never pursues her fated mate, she can still find contentment with many partners. It's not an issue for us if a Fae chooses to stay single, or if they just enjoy a constant rotation of partners. It only becomes a problem when a

Fae chooses to accept and claim their fated mate. Then there are different rules."

"Fascinating." Bianca pursed her lips, interest dancing in her eyes. "I've been keeping up with my research, but I still have so much to learn. So basically, you all are like, sure and let's sleep with anyone under the sun, but once you've made your claim, it's time to be a prude."

"Not a prude, no, as you'll make love with your fated mate," Terra said. "It's because of the extra magicks you get when you combine your union. The Fae are protective of that. Maybe it's not the best rule, and perhaps exile is a bit extreme. It wouldn't hurt for the royals to look at revising some of their punishments."

"I'd say." Bianca shook her head. "It's a very dramatic response. Plus, how come the wife wasn't exiled but the lover is?"

"Also a good question that I cannot answer," Terra agreed with Bianca. It had always rankled her a bit that Eoghan's wife got to stay in the Fae Realm while Rian had to walk away. Rian hadn't been the one to make vows.

"What if we align ourselves with Rian first? If we say we believe him ... wouldn't that help us to sway him to our side? He'd feel like he has allies already?" Bianca asked.

Terra leaned back and crossed her arms over her chest. She cast her mind back to Rian's trial, and the subsequent turmoil that resulted from his prosecution. It was the look in his eyes before he'd been dragged away that had caused her to try and investigate further. At the time, Terra hadn't known that Rian was her fated mate. That information had only been revealed to her later after she'd heard her heartsong on the wind for the first time. It had taken her several attempts, but finally her powerful magick combined with her scrying stream had revealed Rian to be her mate. But before then? She'd already been investigating his crime further, a part of her suspecting there was more to the story than had been revealed.

Her brother had been furious.

Their ugly encounter had fractured their family, with the majority taking sides with Eoghan and his fury over Terra's line of questioning. When she'd refused to drop it, continuing to investigate further even after Eoghan had ordered her to stop, he'd stopped speaking to her. Cormac, her other brother, had sided with Eoghan, telling Terra that her power as leader of the Earth Fae had gone to her head, while her parents had done their best to remain neutral even though Terra could sense their disapproval. Unfortunately, as a leader, Terra didn't get the luxury of only making decisions that she felt comfortable with. Eventually, her queries had met with enough dead ends that she'd had to abandon the cause as greater issues had demanded her attention.

Like the Domnua trying to overthrow their power.

"I don't know whether I believe him or not," Terra said, returning to the conversation. "But I did search for more information after he was exiled, and I think he might be telling the truth. There was something in his eyes on the day he was exiled that made me want to look further for more information. I didn't find any, which, I suppose is inconclusive on whether Rian is innocent or not. And, well, I spent a lot of time with his mother after he was exiled. She had nobody else, and her health was failing. From what she'd said of Rian, from every appearance, he was a really lovely man. It about broke her heart that he'd been exiled. I did my best to be a comfort to her in her last days. But, that being said, I'm not sure I'm capable of pretending something if I don't know if it is true or not. I mean, people are capable of anything, aren't they? I guess ... your plan could be tricky for me. Not to mention it's a really upsetting subject matter for him. Look how far he's already gone to seek revenge on us. It feels like kicking a wasp's nest, no?"

"That's a good point. You're more than likely to just infuriate the man further. Right, so we're back to a good old-fashioned wooing. Here's what we do... you use your feminine wiles, your nurturing aspect, and your sweet nature to draw him in. He needs someone to be vulnerable with as he's hurting. That person has to be you."

"And if we accomplish this? And he falls in love with me? How will he feel if he finds out we planned it?" Terra looked out the window where the sun dipped to the horizon.

"Will it matter? If you both love each other and you're happy? You could tell him you did it for his own good because you could see what he needed in his life."

Oh. *Right*.

Terra hadn't considered the aspect of *her* falling in love, and she held the idea up in her mind, twisting it from all angles to look at what it would mean for her, while her heart shivered in her chest. Had it only taken his kiss to already tip her over the edge into love? Already she understood that she would put her life on the line for this man, which she'd heard was one of the most compelling aspects of being in a fated mate union.

Maybe, just maybe, this plan might be the answer they needed.

"Yes, Bianca. Let's do this. Tell me what you're thinking..."

8

LATER THAT EVENING, after Terra had all but worn a path across her cottage from her pacing, she gave up and knocked lightly at her door. Within a few moments, the door opened quietly, and moonlight spilled inside the cottage.

"Yes, Lady Terra?" Callahan asked politely.

"I understand your duties to Rian, and that I am being held as a captive. However, I'm not used to being inside." Terra gestured at the stone walls. "It's ... well, I'm very restless and unable to sleep. Is it possible that I might go for a walk? If I give you my word that I won't try to escape or bring any harm upon myself or others?"

Callahan regarded her carefully as he considered her words. Would his loyalty to Rian forbid him from breaking the rules, or would he trust her to do as she promised?

"A walk it is, my lady. If you'll please be cautious in your step, as there are many steep cliffs nearby, and not wander too far, I certainly don't see a problem with you taking in some fresh air."

"Thank you." Terra squeezed his arm as she slipped past him, surprised by the buzz of energy that she got from touching him. The man was much more powerful than just a butler, Terra realized, and she flashed Callahan a knowing look.

"Fire Fae," Callahan said, an easy smile on his lips.

"Ah yes. You conceal it well."

"Habit, I suppose. Living among humans causes you to mask constantly, and you get better at it the longer you do so. I suppose that can be said for many things we mask, can't it?" Callahan gave her a small smile before fading discreetly into the background as Terra gulped the fresh night air as though she was a drowning woman coming up from the depths for a breath. She paused, closing her eyes as the cool night air filled her lungs, and the moonlight bathed her face in its caress. The sound of the waves hitting the cliffs far below was more prominent now that she was outside and, drawn to the water, she followed a path that led away from the cluster of buildings. The moon was full this night, and she itched to take her dress off and perform her usual full-moon rituals. Maybe she would, though she'd left her pack with her tools back at the cottage. The knife pulsed at her thigh, happy as she was to be out in the wilds again, and she felt the tension ease from her shoulders.

Granted, Terra understood that she was in a predicament. However, there was no use in trying to escape. Not when they were isolated on an island with the very man she'd sought to find and deter from his evil plans. The situation may have changed, but the players were still the same. Now Terra just needed to play the new game, while seeking to shift Rian's focus. According to Bianca, most men were similar in their desires, and Terra shouldn't have much problem distracting Rian. Terra wasn't so sure. Rian was a powerful warrior in his own right, and he'd likely be well versed in sniffing out and avoiding any obstacle that got in the way of his goal.

And destroying it.

With those thoughts on a loop in her mind, Terra stopped at a small beach with the tiniest strip of sand, that led to a miniscule channel between several high pillars of rocks. No boat would be able to approach there, and Terra was beginning to understand why Rian had chosen this location. A flash of silver in the water caught her eye.

But that didn't mean the Water Fae couldn't reach it.

When the Fae lifted his head from the water, the moonlight glinting off his opalescent eyes, Terra bowed her head to him.

"Sister."

"Brother," Terra said, acknowledging the Fae. "How are your people?"

"Concerned. We've been sent to try and find you. King Callum is distraught. Will you come with me?" The Water Fae swam closer, the moonlight glinting off the dark water surrounding him. Terra glanced over her shoulder to where she could just see the small cluster of buildings up on the hill over where she stood. A lone light shone from a window in one of the outer buildings, and she wondered if Rian was awake.

If he thought of her as much as she thought of him.

"I can't go with you brother. I'm still needed here. Please tell King Callum that I am safe for now. I'll try to check back with you when I can."

"Do you require our people to stay close?"

Terra thought about it. On one hand, it would be wise to have the help if needed, but she wasn't quite ready to call in the troops. Unless the Domnua attacked — then she might be thinking differently.

"As of now, I do not, but if a few can remain close in case of need? Perhaps to bring messages back to the king?"

"As you wish." The Fae slipped beneath the water, becoming nothing more than a shimmer of silver below the surface, and Terra continued her trek up a narrow path that led to a grassy meadow and ended at a steep drop-off into the dark ocean far below. Terra stepped carefully back from the edge, remembering her promise to Callahan, and turned in a circle. From here, she could no longer see the settlement, and she felt free to indulge herself in a small full-moon ritual. Carefully, she knelt and slipped off her soft boots that melded seamlessly to her feet, and unlaced the ties of her dress, before pulling the silky material over her head. With a sigh of relief, Terra stood, naked but for the knife strapped to her thigh, and smiled up at the moon.

This was all she really needed to be happy, Terra reminded herself. The kiss of moonlight, the salty night air, and her feet dug into the springy moss of the Earth. Already she could feel her power recharging, as though the Earth itself fed her its energy, and she stretched her arms up to the sky.

"Mother moon, the most graceful artisan of our night skies, thank you for blessing us with your light."

"What are you doing out here?"

Terra whirled at the sharp words, her moon gratitude ritual interrupted, and gaped at Rian who stepped closer. His eyes gleamed in the moonlight, and his face was all sharp edges and shadows.

"I ... I struggle with being inside. I needed some fresh air." Terra was immediately aware of two things. The first? Her body seemed to come alive under his unwavering gaze. And the second? The knife he sought was clearly visible strapped to her thigh. She'd miscalculated, and now Terra waited to see what Rian's next move would be. Gathering her power inside of her, she put her hand to the hilt of her blade. It didn't matter the move would draw his attention, it was better to be prepared.

His eyes flitted to the knife at her thigh, and she watched as he drew in a ragged breath, his chest shuddering with the effort.

"Why are you always naked?" Rian all but growled as he prowled closer, circling her, and forcing her to turn with his movements in order to track him.

"I'm not *always* naked. But it's my preferred state of being when I'm alone in the wilds. Do you have a problem with nudity?" The Fae weren't modest, and clothes were oftentimes an afterthought depending on the situation. They didn't attach any moral value to being clothed or not, though the wearing of clothes was the more common choice among most Fae. Quite simply because the Fae loved beautiful things, and elaborate dress adorned with gold or sparkly accessories appealed to their love of all things flashy.

"No, I don't have a problem with nudity. I have a problem with *you* always being naked." Rian ran a hand through his hair, frustration in his voice.

Interesting. Terra was reminded of Bianca's point about how simple men could be at times. Was her body driving him to distraction? Would he be overcome with lust like he'd been earlier that day? Curious, she stepped closer to him and was shocked to see him take a step back.

"You told me that you liked my body, if I remember correctly? Has that changed? Also, you'll have to teach me your spell for how you were able to transport just the image of yourself without being in the same place. Fascinating, really..." Terra trailed off as Rian gaped at her.

"This is not ... we're not..." Rian sputtered. "You are my *captive*. We aren't friends exchanging recipes here, Terra."

"Right, right. It's just that I find what you did so fascinating, and I'm genuinely interested in learning from you." Terra tried batting her eyelashes at him as she remembered Bianca's advice about trying to flatter Rian.

"Is something wrong with your eyes?" Rian asked, confusion crossing his face. He kept a healthy distance between the two of them, and Terra couldn't help but wonder who was really the captive here?

"Yes, just a bit of the salt in the air," Terra said. *Eyelash fluttering was out. Noted.*

"Put your dress back on and come with me. You shouldn't be this close to the cliff's edge."

"I'd like to finish my ritual," Terra said, digging her toes into the ground.

"This isn't about what you'd like, princess. We're not at a spa or some yoga retreat. What you want is irrelevant. Understood? The earth doesn't care about your stupid rituals. Nobody..." Rian broke off, but Terra already knew what he was going to say. That nobody cared.

Because *he* thought that nobody cared about him. Bianca was right. The man was all but crying out for love. She'd have to be patient with Rian but, luckily, as leader of the Earth Fae, Terra understood patience in a way that many did not. She took her lessons from nature, where sometimes change could take thousands of years to enact. Quickly, she stepped forward and put her hand to Rian's chest, feeling the beating of his heart beneath the soft flannel shirt he wore. Rian stared at her, disbelief and something deeper moving behind his gaze.

"I'm sorry you're hurting," Terra said, infusing love and concern into her touch, so that a soft rush of energy left her palm and flowed to him. Rian grabbed her hand, breaking the connection with his heart, and gripped it almost tightly enough for her to wince.

"I'm not hurting. Don't you understand, princess? I don't feel anything at all." Rian bit the words out, as though she couldn't see past his lies, his face haggard in the moonlight.

"I don't believe you," Terra whispered. The moment stretched out, and Terra thought maybe, just maybe, she might be breaking through to him. She could see as he struggled for control.

"That's just fine. I'm used to nobody believing me, remember?" The words hit her like a whip and, before she could retort, his lips were on hers.

She wanted his kiss. Goddess, but she wanted him, but not like this. As his fury poured into her, she matched him with her own intensity, trying to use her light to push back his darkness. They fueled each other, Rian hitching one of her legs around his waist, and cupping his hands around her bum. He squeezed her soft flesh so tightly, Terra was certain she'd have bruises. And still she didn't break the kiss.

This was a man who needed love, and she was resolved to give it to him in any way that she could. His lips on hers demanded everything, and Terra held nothing back, relishing in the fire that raged between them. It was another lesson from nature that Terra sought now. While nature could be achingly patient, it was often violent and wildly unpredictable at times. Knowing that, she reached between them and cupped his hardness, her grip causing his entire body to tremble beneath her touch. She stroked him, not softly, and laughed when he cursed into her mouth. Frustration was replaced by longing, and soon he thrust into her palm, as Terra pulled him toward completion. When he came, his body shaking beneath her touch, Terra smiled and stepped back, her lips swollen from his kiss.

"I believed you," Terra said, holding his eyes. Her entire body begged for his touch, but she wouldn't allow herself such pleasure. She needed somewhat of an upper hand here, though her path forward was getting cloudier by the minute.

Without another word, Rian turned and stormed away, taking with him the temptation to lie down beneath the moonlight and beg him to worship at her altar. Terra pressed a hand to her lips, still tasting him, and turned her head to the moon. Only then, after she'd centered herself, did she realize that a certain pulse of magick was missing.

Her hand went to her thigh, her heart plummeting, and she swore.

Rian had stolen the amulet, and she only had herself to blame for it. Closing her eyes, she bowed her head and asked for the moon's forgiveness.

9

RIAN STARED at the Earth Fae's knife, turning the blade in his hands, the thrum of power palpable against his palms. This was the culmination of years of focus, and now, if he chose, he could bend their people to his will with this knife. It wasn't like he could demand blind obedience, but the one who carried the amulet commanded the power of the Earth Fae. Already, Rian could sense how carrying such an enchanted item maximized his own power. Strapping the knife to his calf, he finished undressing and waded into the cold stream to wash the day's dirt and grime away.

And the reminder of how quickly Terra had stroked him to spine-tingling joy. No. Not joy. Just pleasure. That was all. He hadn't been with a woman in ages, and Terra was an intoxicatingly beautiful one at that. His hands flexed in the icy water, as though he could still feel her soft curves beneath his palms, and his body twitched in response. She was a walking fantasy, her body made for touching, her mouth a gift. He was certain he could have reached completion from her kiss alone, for there was something about her that made him crave her. The taste of her was like sweet wine, a delicacy to be savored, and somehow he'd allowed her to get the upper hand in that situation.

Well, not entirely.

The knife thrummed at his calf, its power unmistakable, as Rian ducked his head in the dark water and made quick work of rinsing himself. The shock of the icy water against his skin had at first burned, but now as the numbness settled in, Rian focused on that feeling. *Numb* was what he wanted to be. Needed to be. It was easier to make decisions that aligned with his ultimate goal of revenge if he didn't have emotions clouding his vision.

And Terra? She was like a thorn in his side. What he should be doing right now is calling upon the Goddess Domnu and handing the knife over so he could seek his revenge. Instead, Terra's kiss was making him pause and take his time with his next steps. He didn't like the power she held over him. He'd need to change that. In business, when a problem presented itself in a negotiation, Rian didn't always bulldoze his way through. Sometimes he'd step back and have a go at it from another angle, in order to see if there was a different way to get what he wanted.

Now, with Terra, he wondered if there was a way to get more than he'd originally set out for. Could he seek his revenge *and* win her over? The very thought of having Terra sent warmth spiraling through his entire body, and the knife hummed happily at his leg. Annoyed, Rian pushed those thoughts aside and left the stream, using his shirt to towel off his body before rinsing his pants in the water. He had more clothes back at the settlement. Deciding to take a cue from Terra, he walked naked across the field, ignoring how happy the Earth was to have him there, and how the moonlight gently caressed his body. It had been years since he'd walked barefoot in the grass, connecting with the energy of the Earth, and he'd forgotten the rush of power that the Earth Fae would get when touching their bare feet to the ground. No wonder Terra was always naked in the wilds — she was constantly recharging her magick. No matter how much Rian tried to ignore the buzz of power that radiated through him when connecting with the Earth again, he couldn't quite freeze it all the way out.

Part of him wasn't sure he wanted to.

And that was the real problem, wasn't it? Being near Terra was making him think and feel things that didn't align with how he'd structured his world since his exile. Part of the reason he'd done so was because if he could block out the emotions, then he wouldn't be prone to rash decisions or ridiculous fits of anger. Cool, calculated, and controlled was the only way forward.

Callahan waited at the door to his converted cottage, a knowing grin on his face as he took in Rian's appearance.

"You look ... relaxed," Callahan commented, following Rian inside though he hadn't invited the man to do so.

"I was washing the day's grime off. No need to live in my own filth just because we're all but camping out here," Rian bit off.

"Right." When Callahan said no more, Rian turned to

find the man staring at the knife strapped to his calf. Callahan's expression was one of sadness and resignation, though he quickly schooled it when he caught Rian looking at him.

"Do you have something to be saying, Callahan? Out with it," Rian said as he grabbed another pair of pants and tugged them over his legs, concealing the knife from Callahan's watchful eyes.

"You've taken the amulet from Lady Terra ... or did she give it to you?" Callahan asked, his tone crisp around the edges.

"I took it," Rian said. He should feel satisfied by his maneuver, that even though she'd managed to gain the upper hand, quite literally, during their little tryst, he hadn't altogether lost his head. "Any other questions?"

"Of course, sir. What are your plans now that you have it? Will we be moving on shortly then?" Callahan was aware of the plan to hand the Earth Fae's amulet over to the Domnua though he strongly disagreed with it.

"That was the plan, wasn't it?" Rian bit out.

"It was. I'm just clarifying our steps forward and seeing if your plans had changed."

"Why would my plans have changed?" Rian dropped onto a bench and crossed his arms over his bare chest, leveling a questioning look at Callahan. Despite his need to keep his harsh exterior, he couldn't help but soften when he looked at Callahan. The man had been his most loyal friend and had helped him whenever he'd asked for it. Even when Callahan had disagreed with something that Rian was doing, he still stayed by his side. As much as Rian hated being questioned, the man had earned the right to do so.

"Because life is subject to change, isn't it?" Callahan took a seat on the corner of the bed and crossed his legs at the ankles. "I think we both know well enough that our paths can divert in an instant. Will you be handing the knife over?"

"I..." Rian sighed and scrubbed a hand over his face. He wasn't a liar. He could be brutal in his honesty, but he'd still be truthful. "I don't rightly know what I'll be doing yet. I thought the answer would be so simple. Get the knife and revenge is mine. Yet I'm hesitating to make that decision. I don't like it. You know me well enough to know that I prefer a clear path forward. It's like ... I suddenly can't see what was once so clear for me. It's all gotten muddled up in my brain, and I'm not sure what the best choice is."

"You know what I say when things are like that?" Callahan asked, twisting a simple gold band he always wore on his index finger.

"What's that?" Rian suspected he already knew the answer.

"Wait."

When Rian just looked at Callahan with frustration, the old man rocked backwards with laughter.

"Patience, me boy. If you can't see the way out, then give it a little time. Your vision is shrouded for a reason, don't you think? Would you regret handing the knife over before you can see straight?"

"Yes." Rian sighed. "I would regret the decision. It's

not one I make lightly, even though I understand that it could be my path to redemption."

"Give it a few days then. What can change all that much in that time anyway? It's not like the Goddess Domnu expected you to locate the dagger so quickly. It's likely she'll be thinking you're still on a quest to get it. She won't think that forever, but I'm guessing you've got a buffer of a few days before the Domnua start sniffing around. Use that time to gain clarity on your path."

"How?" Rian demanded. "You think absolution lies in this isolated island in the middle of the ocean? What answers could possibly come to me here?"

"Ah, boyo. I've had some choice words for you over the years, but stupid has never been one of them. I'm of the mind to revise that opinion just now though." Callahan stood and crossed to the door.

"Wait, you're calling me stupid and walking away? I thought you were meant to be my trusted advisor. Isn't that your job? To advise?" Rian all but growled in frustration.

"Oh, now I'm an advisor? I thought you introduced me to your friends as a butler. If I'm just a butler, then, I think I've taken care of my duties, haven't I?" Callahan scooped up the wet clothes that Rian had abandoned on the floor. "I'll just see to hanging these out to dry."

"Cantankerous old coot," Rian muttered as Callahan slipped through the door.

"Stubborn young fool," Callahan shot back before the door shut.

Despite his annoyance, Rian grinned after the old man's departure. Callahan was the only man who could speak to him like that and get away with it. It was good for him to have somebody in his life who talked back. The issue was, right now he needed answers, and Callahan was being stubborn about helping him. Which meant the old man wanted him to come up with his own answers. Annoyed, Rian lifted his pant leg and took out the knife, placing it on the table in front of him. It was a relatively unassuming blade, with an emerald hilt that showcased a gilded Celtic design. The blade itself wasn't all that long, but its strength lay in its deception. Many would pass over this blade, thinking it fairly nondescript or not all that powerful, and that was likely a deliberate design. For its true power lay in the magick that coursed through it. Idly, he trailed a finger across the blade, and was instantly rewarded with a cut. A drop of blood dripped from his finger, onto the blade, and the knife began to glow.

Instantly, Rian's mind was cast to Terra and how she'd felt in his arms. Naked, entwined around him, the light of the full moon raining down on them like a benediction. He still remembered the day he'd first seen her up close, angry, terribly beautiful, as she judged him at his trial. She'd never quite left him since, Rian realized, and now her words came back to haunt him.

I believed you.

Had she really? Or was she just saying that because it was the right thing to say in that moment? If she had — why hadn't his exile been overturned? Rian had more questions than answers, and an even bigger one loomed.

Why couldn't he resist Terra? Every time he was near her, it was as though he had to do everything in his power not to touch her. And he'd failed twice now. Either he needed to stay away from her, or he needed to just have his way with her and get her out of his system. There would be no in-between. He'd never been one for dancing in the gray areas of life, and he certainly wouldn't do so now. Either way, Callahan was right. He needed time before he decided what to do with this amulet.

Turning, he lifted a floorboard and pulled out an iron lockbox, ignoring the sting of the metal at his skin. Rian unpacked a charmed cloth from his satchel and carefully wrapped the knife in the cloth, before placing it inside the safe. Not only did he lock it with a code on the little lock on the door, but he also used an intricate spell to protect it. When finished, he swiftly moved the box back beneath the floorboards, and again used his magick to seal the space. Red marks tinged his fingers where he'd touched the metal but, all things considered, it wasn't the worst pain he'd felt that day.

No, that award could go to Terra. Though he'd enjoyed her touch immensely, the pain of not knowing how it felt to be buried deep inside her caused his body to stir again, and he knew it wasn't likely he would get much sleep that night. Resigned to a restless night, Rian dropped onto his bed and pulled a pillow over his head. When his body screamed for release, *again*, he reached for himself with his hand.

When he finally found the relief he sought, it was with Terra's name at his lips.

10

"GOOD MORNING, Lady Terra. I hope you had a restful evening after your walk?"

"Good morning, Callahan." Terra didn't answer his question because her evening had been anything but restful as worry about what Rian planned to do with the amulet had consumed her thoughts. "Will we be able to leave our confines today?"

"Yes, that's why I am here. We have a rare bit of sunshine, so I set up breakfast outside if you'd like to take some air. Oh, and before you do so..." Callahan raised a finger, causing Terra to pause. "It seems that himself has gotten a few wounds on his hands. Perhaps you have something that may help?"

"Is that right? From what, do you know?" Terra was already reaching for her bag where she carried a number of ingredients for her magicks.

"I believe a knife cut and blisters from iron."

"Iron? Why is that fool touching iron?" Terra muttered, digging through her bag.

"He also has not slept. Perhaps something for relaxation as well?" Callahan suggested, and Terra shot him a considering look over her shoulder.

"What's this about, Callahan?"

"Miss Bianca has informed me of a plan of sorts..." Callahan trailed off, steepling his hands in front of him, a pleased expression on his face.

"Is that right? I'm surprised she shared with you. Aren't you meant to be loyal to Rian? How do we know you won't go tell him?"

"Ah yes, a valid question. How best do I say this?" Callahan rocked on his heels and tapped a finger to his mouth. "I'm loyal to Rian's best interests. Sometimes, the man can work against himself if you understand what I'm saying?"

"Sure and I can be understanding the nature of stupid men," Terra grumbled, and then she winced when Callahan's eyebrows rose. "Not all men. Just Rian."

"Of course, Lady Terra. I believe I called him the same myself last night."

"Did you now?" Terra straightened and considered Callahan. "Is Bianca right to think you're on our side then?"

"I don't know that there's sides, necessarily," Callahan said. "At least not between the three of you and Rian, though he sees it differently. However, I *am* on the side of making sure the Dark Fae do not prosper."

"Yet you help him on his mission."

"I do. But make no mistake, Lady Terra. I am not a gentle bystander who follows Rian blindly. I'd like to consider myself more of a guide, really."

"You care for him." A piece of her was glad that Rian had someone in his corner.

"I do." Callahan shrugged a shoulder, unapologetic in expressing his emotions. "But I offer no one blind allegiance, Lady Terra. It's why I left our realm years ago. I'm at peace with my choice to do so. I can only hope Rian finds the same."

"He's the least peaceful man I've ever met," Terra grumbled as she put her ingredients on the table and began mixing a salve for Rian's blisters. At that, Callahan barked out a laugh.

"No, for an Earth Fae, the man does run heated, doesn't he? I'd liken him more to a lightning bolt than a calmly rooted tree."

"Agreed. His roots were ripped out of the ground, weren't they?" Terra pursed her lips as she mixed the salve, pulling at the cord of magick inside of her and infusing the balm with love.

"That's the nice thing about nature, isn't it? Roots have a way of finding a new place to grow." With that, Callahan left her to finish her preparations, leaving the door propped open with a stone. The sound of voices drifted inside on the sea breeze and, at any other time, Terra would have relaxed into an easy morning of making magickal remedies with some of the finest earthly ingredients. Today, though, she hurried herself along, not wanting to miss the chance to pamper Rian a bit.

The jerk.

It still stung, that he'd slipped the knife from her so easily, and she was beginning to understand the danger of the fated mate bond. It was as though she couldn't think straight or was conscious of anything else when she was wrapped in his arms. It rankled, it did, that he'd been able to still formulate a plan while she'd brought him pleasure. Did that mean he didn't have the same powerful attraction for her that she had for him? Insecurity was an unfamiliar emotion for Terra, so the thought was more confusing than upsetting, though she'd dearly like an answer. From the looks of Rian's expression when she stepped from her cottage, Terra immediately ascertained she'd not be getting answers today. He stood at the end of the table, head bent to Callahan, a furious expression on his face as he pointed at the food and then at Bianca and Seamus. Terra didn't have to hear what he was saying to know he disapproved.

Even with storm clouds in his expression, Rian looked handsome, and Terra's heart sighed at the sight of him. Today he wore dark pants and a simple flannel shirt in heather green, and the color highlighted his moody eyes. She wanted to go give him a hug, even though she was angry with him. It was such a confusing thing, this fated mate feeling, Terra realized. How was it possible to be angry with someone and want to care for them at the same time? Perhaps that was the contradiction that came with true love. It unsettled her, this thought of love, and she dropped to a seat across from Bianca and Seamus instead of greeting Rian. She needed to work up the nerve to talk to him, because at the moment, anything from "take me" to "you stupid jerk" was bound to come out of her mouth.

"Have there been some developments we aren't aware of?" Bianca asked, leaning into Seamus's side.

"Good morning, Terra." Seamus grinned at her.

"Good morning. Yes, well, let's see... I went for a walk. Rian and I, we ... had a moment. And he stole the amulet. That's a quick synopsis of recent events," Terra said, narrowing her eyes at Rian. Anger with him seemed to be winning over lust, so that was a good sign at least. Maybe she'd be able to focus that anger into something productive like stealing her amulet back. But ... it didn't feel like the knife was nearby. Terra was so in tune with the knife that she could usually feel the pulse of its energy when it was close, and now ... nothing. Dread slipped its icy fingers into her gut.

"What have you done with the amulet?" Terra asked, her voice sharp, causing Rian to snap his head up. "Please tell me you haven't been so absolutely asinine as to have given it to the Dark Fae?"

"There you go ... insult him. That'll make him fall for you," Bianca whispered.

Terra didn't care about their plans in that moment. Rage bubbled inside her, and her magick responded, growing heavier as it rippled through her. She wasn't sure what she would do if Rian told her that he'd given the knife away.

"I have not given the amulet to the Dark Fae," Rian said. He narrowed his eyes at Terra, like she was the problem, his face set in hard lines.

"Where is it then?" Terra demanded. Rian was presenting her with quite a problem. On one hand, he'd told her repeatedly that he didn't lie and became furious when people didn't believe him. On the other, if Terra didn't believe his words now, any tenuous foundation they were starting to build would be shattered.

"I've tucked it away. In a safe place." Rian's hands jerked, almost inadvertently, and Terra understood now why he had the wounds. He must have put the amulet somewhere surrounded by iron, which would protect it from the Dark Fae, as well as insulate its powers. That must be why she couldn't feel its presence nearby.

This was also an opportunity to show Rian she was willing to trust him. Even though he'd stolen the amulet from her. It stung, knowing that she had put herself out there for him, while he was still committing wrongs against her. But she also understood now that, in some respects, Rian wasn't just seeing Terra as herself. As a leader of the Earth Fae, she represented the group that had punished him so harshly. It was her duty to accept his censure, particularly if he was innocent, which meant now was a perfect time to start building that bridge back to him. Standing, Terra picked up her jar of salve, and a small bag of loose tea she'd mixed to help Rian rest. Callahan stepped back when Terra moved to Rian, giving them space.

"What? Don't believe me?" Rian taunted, regarding her with weary eyes.

"Let me see your hands," Terra said, and surprise flitted across Rian's face.

"No," Rian said, starting to step back, but Terra had anticipated his retreat and was already reaching for his wrist. At her touch, he stopped in his tracks, as though she held some kind of power over him. Which, if last night was any indication, wasn't as much as she'd origi-nally thought. Turning his right hand over in her palm, Terra grimaced at the large blisters she found there. Had the man not even tried to protect himself from the pain? "It's nothing—"

"Hush." Terra ordered, and rubbed some salve onto his wounds, taking some time with the motion in order to take the pain from his flesh and into herself. Being bare-foot, she could direct the pain through her and into the ground, where the Earth helped her to disperse the energy. "There ... that should be a bit better."

Rian looked down at his palms and back to her, his face still set in a scowl, confusion in his eyes. He reminded Terra of a wounded animal needing care, but suspicious of any help that was offered. That was just fine. She was more than used to healing the wounds of the world. Rian would just be one more animal in her menagerie.

"I have a tea for you," Terra said, handing him the small bag.

"Tea?" Rian asked in a tone that sounded like he was certain she was trying to poison him.

"For restless sleep. It works wonders." Terra patted his arm before he could move out of the way of her touch and returned to her seat where Bianca was scooping porridge into a bowl for Terra.

"It's a nice morning, all things considered," Seamus commented, gesturing with a spoon to the sunny sky.

"It is at that," Bianca agreed, hyperaware of where Rian stood frozen at the end of the table, gaping at them. "Should we have a walk later? Or perhaps a game?"

Bianca asked. She turned and addressed Rian. "Would you like some porridge? There's plenty here."

"Would I like..." Rian trailed off, his face mutinous, as he turned on his heel and stormed to his cottage. Terra noticed that he'd taken the bag of tea with him, so perhaps that was a modicum of progress.

"I guess he's not hungry." Bianca winked at Terra.

"I suspect your man is feeling like he's losing control of things," Seamus commented as Callahan joined them at the table. A gull swooped in wide arcs over their heads, curious at what they were eating, and the sound of the waves hitting the rock walls carried to them across the meadow. It was as peaceful a moment as any could be while being held captive, Terra supposed. Turning, she looked at Callahan.

"What's stopping us from using our magick? None of us have been disarmed." Terra pointed a finger at the other two. "Like ... this is the most lackadaisical prison I've ever come across."

"Sure it is at that." Callahan chuckled and scooped up some porridge. "The truth of it is that you can't swim from here, a boat can't access the shores safely, and Rian has put enough bloody wards on the island to stop you from transporting out. You can still use your magick, but you'd just be firing it off at each other, really."

"We can't use it to force Rian to break the wards?" Bianca leaned in, her blue eyes going icy.

"Could do." Callahan shrugged. "But it's likely he's built in a fail-safe where the magick can't be disarmed under duress. He's highly skilled."

"Then we just have to wait here ... in this in-between

... while Rian figures out what to do with his personal vendetta against the Earth Fae?" Bianca summarized quickly.

"It seems that way, yes," Callahan said.

"Well, now, that's annoying isn't it?" Bianca glanced at Seamus.

"It is my darling beautiful wife. It is. But, we have been saying we've wanted a bit of a vacation, so why not enjoy this nice weather while we have the time to do so? You know, seize the day and all that? We'll be back to battle soon enough from the sounds of it," Seamus said. He dropped a kiss on Bianca's cheek when she pouted.

"What did you have in mind to pass the time, Seamus?"

"Well, I'm kind of a geek, and I've been missing my games. How about we take my lovely wife's suggestion? Shall we have a game of magicks? Maybe a competition?" Seamus's eyes gleamed, and Terra began to understand there were more depths to this man than she had realized. Because if there was one thing she had learned about men from having brothers, is that they loved to compete. Terra's gaze drifted to Rian's cottage and then back to Seamus.

"I think a competition is an excellent idea, Seamus. What did you have in mind?"

11

LAUGHTER GREETED him when Rian stepped back outside, and he stopped short, annoyance making his shoulders hunch. They were supposed to be his captives. And here it looked like Callahan was running a damn summer camp.

"Watch out," Seamus shouted as a stone zoomed toward Rian's head. Rian grabbed it out of midair, narrowing his eyes as he realized that Seamus was using magick for his game, and turned to the group that stood in the meadow in front of the table where they'd had breakfast. The good weather held, and only a few clouds dotted the sky. It wasn't particularly warm, not that Ireland ever was all that warm, but it wasn't horribly freezing either. A perfect day for what looked to be some sort of competition.

Which would be fine and all if they were on a holiday away together and enjoying lawn games and drinks. But that is not what this was. Rian opened his mouth to speak, when another rock zoomed near his head, almost slicing his cheek, and he narrowed his eyes at Terra who had a mischievous glint in her eyes.

Goddess how he wanted her.

When she'd walked out of her cottage this morning, her hair a riot around her shoulders, her lush curves moving fluidly under her silky dress, he'd almost dropped to his knees. The punch of her was so powerful that he'd done the only thing he could think of — scowl and close down. He was waiting for her wrath and, instead, he'd been treated with kindness. Rian's hands clenched involuntarily as he remembered her cooling touch against his skin. She'd healed him, taking in his own pain — that he'd brought upon himself for stealing from her — and he'd just stood there like an idiot unable to form a coherent sentence. Too many emotions had broken loose inside of him, rattling around like broken parts in a box, and he didn't know what to do with them.

So he'd stood there, silently, while she'd treated him more kindly than he had treated her. Terra was making it increasingly difficult for him to hate the Earth Fae.

"You did that on purpose," Rian called, walking closer to where the group huddled.

"Maybe that's the game," Terra said cheekily. "See how close we can get to hitting you without harming you. It's great fun."

"Game?" Rian asked, incredulous. Despite his determination to try and stay away from Terra until he could get his thoughts straight, he moved closer to her like an ant following a sweet trail of sugar.

He could still taste her kisses on his lips.

"Yes, a game. Seamus has challenged us to a bout of magicks. Care to join us?" Terra's smile was both welcoming and hesitant, as though she also was uncertain about his response. Could he blame her? He'd stolen from her as she'd given him the most intense pleasure of his life. The thought of it brought shame, and it was a confusing mix of emotions — the wanting of Terra and embarrassment for having betrayed her at such a vulnerable moment. Rian didn't like it. He didn't like any of this. The day his mother died was the day he'd iced over his emotions for good, and this crack in his carefully built wall was more than disconcerting for him.

He feared it would change the one purpose that had kept him going over the past few desperate years. Where would he be without it? Lonely and an exile. Bitterness washed through him, and he opened his mouth to speak when Bianca laughed, causing him to break his focus on Terra. He glanced over to see Bianca beaming up at Seamus, the two whispering something to each other as lovers do, and his heart twisted.

He wanted *that*.

Before his exile, before his mother had become sick, Rian had been an easygoing man who'd enjoyed teaching. He'd thrived on learning new magicks, often staying up late testing new spells, and loved nothing more than seeing his students' faces light up in wonder when they'd mastered a new trick. He'd never had grand aspirations for himself, because he'd already been living a life he loved. Head of Magicks for the Earth Fae, a few good friends, and the only thing missing had been a partner to make it whole. Sure, he'd enjoyed the company of many ladies through the years, but none had quite fit. None had captivated him the way that Terra had with one burning glance during a trial of his peers. She'd never left him since, and it was a mixture of both relief and dismay to once more be in her presence.

Wait.

Callahan's words from the night before came back to him. Give it time, the man had suggested and, while Rian wanted to ignore where his thoughts took him, he couldn't. As he'd adamantly told Terra — he *wasn't* a liar. Which meant, he couldn't lie to himself either. Rian wanted to spend more time with Terra, and if Callahan thought it was best to wait before he made a move on delivering the knife to Goddess Domnu, then now was his opportunity to explore this magnetic pull that Terra had upon him.

"Sure, I'll play your game." When Terra's mouth dropped open in surprise, it took everything in his power not to lean over and have a taste. "What are the rules?"

"Alright! He's in," Seamus said, stepping forward with several rocks in his hand. "We're trying a new variation next. One of us will throw this stone out into the meadow, and then we each take turns trying to get our own stones closest to it. The trick is that the rest of us can use any magicks we see fit to divert your stone, so you'll need to be ready to defend or counterattack. Once a stone lands on the ground, it can't be moved. So no trying to blow up a stone after it isn't in play anymore, got it?"

The heat of competition warmed his blood, and Rian pushed his sleeves up, eagerly accepting a handful of stones from Seamus. He used to love playing games like these with his students as it encouraged them to think on their feet which would be required of them when they used magick in day-to-day life.

"Mine to go," Bianca called, heaving a larger stone out into the meadow where it bounced and rolled to a stop. Callahan stepped forward. Apparently, he was next to go, and he jiggled the stones in his hand as he considered his tactics. He nodded to himself, as though he'd come to a decision, and then launched a stone into the air and immediately lit it on fire as it flew toward the rock. Rian smiled and played one of his favorites—coating the rock in ice and having it drop to the ground a ways short of the mark. He grinned when Callahan shot him an evil look and was surprised when a ripple of … enjoyment coursed through him. When was the last time he had truly enjoyed anything?

"What are we playing for?" Rian asked, competition heating his blood. Turning, he surveyed the others.

"Would it be too cheeky to play for our release?" Bianca asked, a hand on her hip.

"Yes, because if I win, where does that put me?" Rian countered, tossing a stone in the air and catching it.

"That's fair, I suppose. How about we get a gift from one of the others — within reason?" Seamus asked.

"A gift? Like I could play to win my amulet back?" Terra said, glaring at him, though her tone was teasing.

"Within reason," Rian said. How could she joke about him stealing the knife? Was she forgiving him or dare he even hope, understanding of his motives for doing so? Warmth bloomed, along with a narrow thread of suspicion. Terra was a puzzle, and one he was slowly becoming determined to figure out.

"Fine. But I'm motivated now," Terra warned him. Her luscious lower lip stuck out in a pout, and Rian wanted to lean over and bite it. Turning before his body betrayed his attraction to her, Rian stood back as the others took their turns at trying to stop Callahan's progress. He didn't want to reveal all of his tricks too early in the game.

The others took to the game with enthusiasm, and he found himself biting back laughter at their increasingly absurd attempts at stopping the others' stones from nearing the marker. Seamus was up and, while Rian contemplated if he should step in, Bianca beat him to it.

Sidling close to Seamus, Bianca reached around and cupped him between the legs just as the man launched his stone into the air. Cursing, Seamus jumped, and his stone dropped to the ground a foot in front of him.

"Simple, but effective," Bianca said with a sly grin on her face. At that, Rian laughed out loud, as Seamus bent to his wife.

"This is a game of magicks. That wasn't magick, you cheeky woman."

"I thought you always told me that my touch is magick?" Bianca forced her lower lip out in a pout. Seamus threw up his hands and sighed, glancing at Rian.

"Well, now, I'm screwed either way if I answer that wrong, aren't I?" Seamus grumbled, and Rian's grin stretched his face wide. The movement was unfamiliar, and he couldn't remember the last time he'd smiled like this. Goddess, but when had his life taken such an unhappy turn?

Be happy.

Remembering his mother's words to him, Rian quenched the feelings of sadness that threatened to rise. He hadn't quite fulfilled his promise to her, had he? Instead, he'd let his quest for revenge dominate his thoughts. Maybe there was another way, a different path forward, but now Rian wondered if it was too late to change his direction. He'd already set the wheels in motion by agreeing to Goddess Domnu's demands. Had he lit a match to his own house? The Earth Fae had decided he was bad, so he'd made the choice to lean into it. Why not accept their judgment of him? But now, watching the wind dance through Terra's hair and the way her smile bloomed on her face like a flower in the first brush of morning sun, his stomach twisted. A week ago he'd been so certain of his choices, and he didn't like second-guessing himself.

Terra surprised him by tossing her stone with very little lead-up, and he scrambled to react. Ice was his go-to, and he grinned as the stone froze and started to drop.

Only to be lit on fire as it flew toward the marker. Was that Callahan counteracting his spell? Glaring at the old man, Rian started when Terra chuckled, her stone landing the closest to the marker.

"Was that you counteracting my spell?" Rian demanded, stepping closer to look down at the beaming Terra.

"You're not the only one strong in magicks, boyo." Terra quirked an eyebrow at him, and then, pursing her lips, she studied the marker once more.

Oh, it was *on*.

This time, when Terra let her stone loose, Rian was ready. Calling upon the air element, he used the power of the wind to divert the stone so far across the meadow that it almost fell over the edge of the cliff.

Almost.

At the last moment, a gull swooped in and captured the stone from its descent and flew it toward the marker. Rian's mouth dropped open as the gull let go of the stone and it fell to the ground, gently rolling toward the marker.

"Yes!" Terra exclaimed, shooting her closed fist in the air. "Didn't think to ask our feathered friends for help, did you?"

"Is that even fair?" Rian demanded. "Isn't that getting extra help from a player who isn't in the game?"

"There's nothing in the rules here about help from animals," Seamus said, pretending to open an imaginary scroll and read it. "Nope, nothing that I can see here in the rules of a game we just made up an hour ago. Animal assistance is allowed."

"Hardly a fair judge," Rian grumbled.

"Oh don't be a poor sport just because I think more quickly than you." Terra shocked him by poking his ribs and then blowing him a kiss as she stepped back so he could take his turn.

"You weren't thinking quickly last night when I was kissing you," Rian said, stopping short of adding ... *when I stole your knife.* But the meaning was clear, and two spots of color bloomed on Terra's cheeks. Good. That meant he got in her head a bit, and her anger would work to her detriment on his round. It was all part of the game, Rian reminded himself, and he could use their emotions to his advantage.

"Damn, Terra. He's asking for it. You'd better not let him win," Bianca said.

"Oh, I'm on it," Terra hissed at his side, and Rian found himself grinning again. It was silly, really. Just a stupid game. And yet he found himself completely invested in the outcome because he already knew what he'd ask for when he won.

Pressing his lips together, Rian hummed to himself as he considered his approach. He needed to get closer than Terra and would need some sort of shield above the stone in case she brought her bird friends back. Nodding his head to himself, he threw the stone along with a domed ice saucer to shield it from any attacks from the sky. Just as his stone neared the marker, grass reached from the ground and snatched the stone from the air, curling it to the ground in a tangle of knots and weeds.

"Oh, come *on*." Rian turned on Terra who was outright laughing at him now. "The grass wasn't even tall enough to reach the stone."

"It's amazing how fast it can grow. Nice climate for it and all." Terra pursed her lips and studied the meadow as though she was a farmer commenting on the crops. Rian refused to let this be the end for his turn and, summoning his power, he called upon the Earth — something he hadn't done in ages. At first, he thought nothing would happen, as maybe the Earth had turned its back on him much like his people had. But, seconds later, the ground rumbled beneath them, and they all gasped as the meadow shook lightly and his stone rolled past Terra's to be the closest to the marker.

"That's not fair. No way. The stone was on the field. It wasn't in play anymore." Terra whirled on Seamus as though he was the official rule keeper. Seamus looked down at Bianca who just shrugged. Lifting his hands in the air, he mimicked unrolling the imaginary scroll again.

"I'm sorry, Terra, but it looks like that falls within the rules. You'll have to work extra hard this round."

"But how? His stone is already closest." Terra jabbed the air with one finger, her beautiful forehead crinkled in frustration. Rian liked seeing this side of her, just a bit wild and frustrated, as though she also had flaws instead of being some gorgeous calm all-knowing Earth goddess. Maybe this could be *his* new personal game — riling Terra up.

"You'll have to use his stone to knock his other one away," Bianca mused as she tapped a finger against her mouth. "Or call your gull back. That might help."

"Wow, are you all ganging up on me then?" Rian turned back to the marker and shook his head sadly at the field. "It's always the way of it, isn't it? Nobody likes losing to the best."

"Oh, would you listen to that ego?" Terra fumed. "You're certainly not the best. You can't even be the best at a game we just made up."

"When I win this, I will be. And you'll be my prize." Rian pointed out, leveling a look at her that was both full of cockiness and heat. It served to unravel her further, which was exactly Rian's intent, as annoyance flashed like lightning in those pretty eyes of hers.

"I most certainly will not—"

Rian was already launching his stone, hoping to catch her off guard, and had put an added layer of protection around the rock, hoping it would stay its course. Just as it neared the marker, the stone exploded.

Rian's mouth dropped open, and he fisted his hands on his hips.

"Terra! You can't just destroy another man's stone."

"Well, I did." Terra crossed her arms over her chest and glared at him.

"That's cheating." Rian looked at Seamus who held up his hands as though to say they needed to work it out between themselves. "Oh come on, man. I know the game is just made up, but destroying someone else's stone completely has to be cheating, right? Otherwise we would've all done that from the beginning."

"Um, well, I suppose..." Seamus trailed off when Bianca stepped forward, a calculating look on her face.

"It doesn't much matter, does it? Rian's other rock is still the closest to the marker. Terra destroyed the wrong rock."

"Oh, you're right." Terra stomped a foot on the ground, sending her lovely breasts bouncing, and Rian was hypnotized for a moment while she had a little tantrum. This side of Terra fascinated him, and if all of this ... movement ... went with her anger, well, he was determined to make her angry more often. She was a captivating woman sitting still, however when in motion, particularly when Terra was angry, well, she was riveting. He didn't care what the rules were anymore, it was time for him to claim his prize. "I hate it. But you're right. I let this one get to me."

Rian wanted nothing more than to get to her. Over and over, hopefully.

"Am I declared the winner?" Rian asked. He waited, unduly invested in the outcome of this silly game.

Bianca glanced at Seamus and then turning, she walked over to the table and returned with something in her hands. When she stopped in front of him, Rian realized she'd made a wildflower chain for the winner to wear.

"Congratulations, Sir Rian, on besting us in this game of magicks. You have won great honor here this day, and you may choose your prize," Bianca said. A cough sounded behind her. "Within reason, of course. And likely nothing involving me, or Seamus may kill you."

Rian bowed his head and accepted the flower chain. It drifted across his face, bringing with it the fresh scent of dirt and clover, and the chain settled softly at his shoulders. Though it was but a silly game, one that he'd actually enjoyed, the flower chain seemed to weigh heavily at his heart. They were treating him as though he was one of the group, accepted, welcomed even. Not like the outcast he was. Or their captor, for that matter. Rian shifted on his feet and refocused on the conversation.

"In the nature of saving ourselves from bloodshed then, I will be choosing the lovely Lady Terra as my prize," Rian said.

"You can't just—"

"An evening," Rian quickly amended. "A date, if you will."

"You're asking me on a date?" Terra demanded, putting her hands into the air and looking around the meadow as though to ask where he planned on taking her for dinner.

"I'm not asking, darling. I'm taking." Rian knew it would anger her and was rewarded when her lovely skin flushed pink and she muttered something beneath her breath.

Likely a murderous threat.

Cheered, Rian turned and walked to the marker. Bending, he pocketed his winning stone, and glanced over his shoulder to see Terra glaring at him.

"I look forward to collecting my prize tonight," Rian called, baiting Terra as he turned and walked toward the cliff's edge where she had given him so much pleasure the night before.

"I'm nobody's prize," Terra yelled after him.

Rian began whistling a cheerful tune and, despite everything, he found himself laughing out loud, the wind tearing the sound from his mouth and carrying it over the cliffs and to the churning waves far below. When he reached the edge of the cliffs, the laughter turned to tears, and he found himself confused by the moisture that dripped down his face.

He'd never cried over the loss of his mother.

Not once. No, anger had ruled there. It was easier to be furious with the Earth Fae than it was to let himself feel the grief he so expertly concealed.

Rian hadn't kept his promise to his mother, nor would his decision to work with the Dark Fae please her. But today? In this moment? He could feel her smiling at him, their energy interconnected through the veil that shrouded life from death, and he understood, once more, just how much she loved him and wanted for him to find his happiness.

Rian hoped it wasn't too late for him to make her proud.

12

A DATE.

Terra couldn't recall ever having gone on an actual date before. Life didn't quite work like that in the Fae realm. Instead, they'd meet lovers during wild celebrations or bond over shared tasks in the village. She'd heard tell of these "dinner dates" the humans loved so dearly, and now Bianca explained more as she braided Terra's hair back from her face.

"So you look at your phone and see a pleasing picture and choose the person you feel like pleasuring that evening? But first, you share food?" Terra squinched her nose in thought, and Bianca laughed.

"That's the way of it, I suppose. Yes, dating apps are quite the rage in the human realm. It takes some of the anxiety out of approaching someone in person. Or, honestly, people are so busy these days. They work long hours and often don't have the time or opportunity to meet new people. The apps can help make connections when you're very busy."

"That is unfortunate. It must be hard to live in a society that demands you work all hours of your day," Terra mused. "Not that I meet many new people either. I spend too much time in the woods. However, I have no problem finding a lover when the need arises."

"I don't doubt it," Bianca murmured, standing back to look at her handiwork. "Just look at you. I'm glad you packed a secondary gown — this is stunning on you."

As an afterthought, Terra had added a gilded gold gown that looked like liquid moonlight. It shimmered and danced with her movements, looking as though someone had poured liquid gold over her curves. At the time, it had seemed a frivolous choice, but now she was happy she'd done so. With no mirror in their accommodation, Terra had to rely upon Bianca's assessment of her look.

"Thank you," Terra said, reaching up to pat her hair.

"I've braided it back on both sides but left it to fall down your back. And I think this will be pretty, no?" Bianca held up a flower crown made of white sea campions and simple yellow buttercups.

"It's lovely, yes."

"It will go nicely against your hair." Bianca bit her lip as she reached up and affixed the flowers to Terra's hair, their sweet scent soothing Terra's nerves.

"Once you find a match, then you have dinner? What do you speak of? Are there rules?" Terra wasn't sure why she was asking. Rian wasn't human, so why would he follow the human culture of dating? Yet he'd lived there long enough now that maybe that was the way he preferred it. If there was a protocol to follow, Terra didn't want to mess anything up. Not only did she need to win Rian over for her people, but also because her fated mate bond sang to her in her soul. Perhaps tonight would be an opportunity to reveal to Rian what they were. It was obvious he hadn't yet pieced together that they were meant for each other, and she wondered if she should sing their heartsong. She voiced the thought to Bianca.

"Sure and I can't be telling you the best way to deal with all that," Bianca said, stepping back once more to glance over Terra's appearance. "However, I might be saving that until we get a better idea of how Rian's going to proceed. You wouldn't be wanting him to think you only brought it up to use against him because he has the knife now, right? If it's meant to be a special thing, it might be best to wait. But you're a good leader, Terra. I'm sure you'll have the best sense of how to be handling things, no?"

"I believe so. I'm just…" Terra gave a small laugh and smoothed her gown. "I'm nervous. And that's not a usual emotion for me to feel. I'm quite confident in my life and the role that I play for our people. It's just…"

"He's a man who has been dealt a difficult hand. Wounded men are…" Bianca sighed and shook her head. "You just want to wrap them up and give them a hug, don't you? Except they'd bite your head off."

"Exactly." Terra started at the knock at the door. "Come in."

"Lady Terra? Your date awaits." Callahan stood at the door and held his arm for Terra as though she was going to a fancy party at the palace. Once outside, Terra's mouth dropped open.

"Well played, man," Bianca whispered behind her.

The meadow was alight with fireflies. They danced and shimmered in a sea of sparkling lights that led all the way to the edge of the cliffs. The sun had just set, silky streaks of pink dashed across the inky sky, and Rian stood at the front of the meadow, in dark pants and shirt, his hair combed neatly back.

In his hands, he held roses.

"This is ... unexpected," Terra murmured.

"I'm working on manners with this one," Callahan said at her side.

"A tricky charge you've undertaken."

"Like a thorn in my side." Callahan laughed. "Too bad I have a dear love for roses. Be gentle with him, Lady Terra. He wears a tough shield, but there's a crack in it."

"I'll take it under consideration."

Callahan released her arm and faded away when they reached where Rian stood, his face immutable, his eyes hawklike as he watched her. She waited for him to hand her the flowers, to move, speak ... to do anything really. When the moment drew out and he just stood there, frozen, she threw up her hands and laughed.

"Is that all there is to this date then? You staring at me in silence?"

Rian jolted, as though suddenly becoming aware of where he was, and jerked his arm forward.

"For you."

"Thank you," Terra said, accepting the small hand-tied bouquet. She wondered if he'd picked the flowers himself. Not likely. A man like him usually had people do things for them. Or did he? It was hard to meld the two versions of Rian she vaguely knew —the Earth Fae's once-respected magicks teacher and a ruthless millionaire businessman in the human realm.

Which man was he tonight?

Rian led her across the meadow to a cluster of trees near the same spot where they'd exchanged their kiss the night before. Did he choose this spot deliberately? Immediately, her mind flashed to how good he'd tasted at her lips.

"I hope this will suit," Rian said, coming to a stop by a carpet that had been laid on the grass beneath the trees with a few cushions scattered across it. At the side, lay a long plank of wood with bowls of fruits and sweets, and a rough-hewn jug of what Terra presumed to be wine. Lights sparkled in the trees above, and Terra's heart sighed. In any other circumstance, this would have been the perfect first date — outside, under the stars, and with an interesting companion. That whole captive thing kind of put a hitch in the romance aspect of all of this, but Terra reminded herself to stick to the plan. It was clear that Rian was confused, and that was something he wasn't used to navigating. She basically had to show him why he needed to side with the Earth Fae once more.

Or even just to be on her side.

Or above her.

Terra shook away the thought of Rian spreading her legs, hovering his body over her, that wicked smile on his lips. A faint flush worked its way across her skin, and she wondered if he had any idea just how attracted to him she was.

"It's lovely here. Sheltered, but not too sheltered,"

Terra said. An ocean-soaked breeze kissing her cheeks was one of Terra's favorite things, and here, where the cliffs jutted proudly out into the sea, was perfect for it.

"Please." Rian took her hand and steadied her as she lowered herself to the carpet. Not that she needed it. Terra's legs were thick with muscles from long days traversing her lands. Nevertheless, the touch of Rian's palm, and the sweet gesture, made her feel just a bit help-less, which was also a feeling that Terra rarely entertained.

Settling the folds of her dress around her legs, Terra waited while Rian sat across from her and stared at her. The silence drew out between them, and Terra was torn on whether to break it herself or allow him to do so. Knowing that silence was often a good tool in a negotia-tion, she decided to wait him out and see what he would lead with. Pasting a small smile on her lips, she relaxed back onto the carpet, propping her head on her hand as she watched him.

"What's your family like?" Rian blurted out, and Terra raised an eyebrow. Interesting. Family must be on his mind, which meant he was likely thinking about the loss of his mother.

"May I?" Terra asked, angling her face at the jug of wine. If she was going to talk about her family, and their difficulties, a little wine would ease the tension.

"Oh, right. I'm sorry. Where are my manners?" Rian shook his head and busied himself with pouring her a glass of rich red wine. There it was again, the contrasts in this man. She was his prisoner and yet he apologized for not pouring her wine. Increasingly, Terra was becoming convinced that Bianca's plan of wooing Rian was the right one.

"Sláinte," Rian said, and handed her a cup. Terra sipped, enjoying the touch of sweetness in the wine, and then met Rian's assessing look.

"I have two brothers. One older than me, and one younger. Eoghan is my older brother and he ... well, he's very reserved. A serious sort. Takes his duties as records keeper seriously. We often butted heads because when I was chosen as the next leader of the Earth Fae, well, I didn't always follow the rules — or issue a rule — in a manner that Eoghan would see fit. He has a particular way of looking at the world. Almost black and white, with very little tolerance for the gray areas of life. He was never one to be all that frivolous or take part in celebrations. His sweet spot is his fondness for animals. He's like me in that respect. Once in a while, he'd join me in the afternoons, and we'd wander in silence through the forest, stopping to greet our animal friends. Those were my favorite times with him before..."

"Before what?" Rian asked, cocking his head, and Terra realized she'd been staring off toward the dark water.

"Ah, well. Eoghan's wife is the one who ... well, she cheated on him. With, well, not you. But..."

"It was your brother?" Rian exclaimed, straightening. His eyes snapped in his face, and Terra's shoulders stiffened.

"It was. That's why I had to stop looking for evidence..." Terra trailed off as Rian swore and looked away, his face mutinous. She was surprised the wine glass didn't crack in his hand, he was fisting it so tightly.

"Cormac is my younger brother," Terra continued when Rian didn't say anything else. At the very least, she might be able to explain the current dynamics of her family and why she'd finally given up on asking questions about Rian's supposed crime. "He's the darling of the family, always smiling, always making everyone laugh. He even managed to make Eoghan cry with laughter at times, and I swear that was what made him happiest. Cormac was always trying to get Eoghan to come play with him, to spend time together but, as they grew older, Eoghan took his duties more seriously. Then he met Marias and, well, Cormac didn't get much of his attention anymore."

"Marias is...?" Rian asked the question so casually, just out of curiosity, really, and Terra's heart sank. She'd been right to push for more evidence in his case, and she'd push harder once she returned to her realm.

"Eoghan's wife," Terra said, her voice soft, acknowledging the unspoken. A ripple of emotion crossed Rian's face, and he threw back the rest of his wine. Terra wasn't sure what to say after that revelation, so she just sipped her wine and waited.

"Did you really look for evidence to help me?" The words sounded like an icicle shattering on the pavement.

"I did." Terra held his eyes, needing him to see the truth in hers. "There was something in your eyes, right before they dragged you away... I just... I couldn't let it go. I asked to have the case reopened, and the high council refused me. Then I started questioning people on my own, as things didn't add up. When my family found out, Eoghan was furious. He'd already had a resolution that fit, you see? He didn't want any other open-ended possibilities being introduced. He and Marias were working on their relationship and were getting to a better place. And Cormac? He might have been even more angry than Eoghan." Terra shook her head at the memory of the last time she'd spoken to Cormac. "It was brutal. He's always looked up to Eoghan, you see? The more I hurt him by keeping the investigation open, the angrier Cormac became with me. We ... we haven't spoken since."

"You what?" Rian leaned forward, shock on his face. "You've stopped speaking with your family?"

Terra shrugged and looked down at her empty mug. She held the glass out to Rian who automatically refilled it for her, his face a mask.

"I would say they've stopped speaking with me, I guess." Terra didn't want to bring up all of the times she'd tried to work on their relationship and had been met with indifference. The ranks had closed, and she was left standing outside. Which was fine, really, as she'd always been a bit more of a loner. Comfortable in the woods and with her animals ... away from having to manage other people's emotions. It made her a good leader, as she wasn't too deeply entwined with any drama among her people, but it could be lonely at times as well.

"How were you chosen? To lead?" Rian's swift change of topic gave Terra pause, and she had to take a deep breath while she moved through the emotions of thinking about her family and the time she'd lost with them.

"Oh, well, it was the mice, really." Terra chuckled at Rian's confused expression. Shifting, she stretched her legs in front of her and smoothed the gold fabric over her thighs. "I've always been able to communicate with things of the earth. Creatures, plants, streams... I feel their energy. I was young, maybe four or five? And I was holding a concert in my garden with several mice in attendance. All lined up in a row, just the way that I wanted them." Terra smiled briefly at the thought of her younger self, enjoying a sunny afternoon with her animal friends. "One of the royals was passing by at the time and took notice. Things moved quickly after that."

"Were you allowed to stay with your family?" Rian asked, drawing Terra's attention back to him.

"Oh, no. Of course not." Terra laughed and smoothed her fingers over her silky skirt. "There was too much training for me to do to be living with my family. I needed to learn all aspects of the Earth Fae in order to lead."

"And your parents ... were fine with this? Couldn't they find another leader or maybe one of the royal bloodline?"

"Oh, we are of the royal bloodline. Just not direct in line to lead." Terra shrugged. "You know the Fae are a matriarchal society, but that doesn't mean it needs to be of the same bloodline. They realized long ago that type of thinking limits the leadership. Not everyone is born to lead."

"But you were." Rian shifted, leaning closer, and Terra found herself doing the same, drawn to him.

"It seems so," Terra said, a small smile on her face. "Mostly, I enjoy it. I feel like I've been able to be a fair leader to our people while still respecting the Earth's needs. It's a fine line to balance."

"If you're the leader, why couldn't you just overturn my exile?" Rian asked. Terra searched his eyes, but found no accusation there, only curiosity.

"In some areas, I am overruled by the Danula Royals. As you well know, they are the supreme rulers of the Elemental Fae, and they lead the High Council. Their decision to do so is because they don't wish to have one person making judgments in cases, which I generally agree with. Except when they get it wrong. Like in your case."

"And your future? What do you see for it?" Terra tried to keep up with his lightning swift changes of topic. It was as though he was spearing small bits of knowledge from her brain and moving on to the next, as if he needed to gather as much information about her as he could. Like they wouldn't have time for such conversations again. And maybe they wouldn't. Terra glanced up at where the trees rustled in the wind from the sea. Was this their moment? Would the Fates give her no more before the events that were set in motion by Rian culminated?

If so, then maybe she needed to act.

"My future?" Terra leaned forward, noticing that Rian subconsciously did the same. "While I'll never be able to live in the confines of the village, that doesn't mean that I don't like people or want to live a life alone. I want a family. A big one, at that. I want happy children that clamber over each other and run wild in the woods with me. I want a partner to curl up with at night and to make love with beneath the stars. I hope to continue to lead our people, fairly and with a strong hand, while not sacrificing my hopes for finding love and creating a joyful family."

"Children?" Rian said the word as though it was foreign to him, rolling the sound around on his tongue, and Terra's breath caught. Would the thought of having a family dissuade him from looking at her in a loving light?

"Yes, children. I ... oh, Rian. There's just something inside me that dearly loves to nurture. I enjoy caring for our Earth, for our wildlife, and being able to be a steady guiding hand for our people. But I'm still missing something. I know that I'm meant to be a mother and that I'll be a good one at that."

"You would be." Rian surprised her by saying. His finger tapped an absentminded rhythm against his wine cup. "I don't know if *I* would be a good father. But I desperately want children as well." Rian said the last bit as though the knowledge surprised him, a revelation that had just appeared to him and he wasn't quite sure what to make of it.

"Our futures are not yet determined," Terra said, choosing her words carefully. Above all else, she could hear the hints of longing hovering over the underlying rage in his voice. Becoming a father was another thing that exile had taken from Rian. "The Fates have their way of directing us, don't they?"

"Is that what you think then? That Fate leads us, and we'll end up where they want us to go?"

"I think the world would be a very neat and tidy place if the Fates had total control." Terra smiled softly at Rian.

"Alas, their power only extends so far. We still choose our path, don't we?"

"In some cases." Rian glowered at her, and Terra sighed. Putting her wine glass aside, she leaned over and took Rian's free hand, a jolt of pleasure racing through her when their skin connected.

"You're right, Rian. You've been wronged, and I'm sorry for that. Truly. Even if I can't get the exile over-turned, will you let bitterness rule your life? Or will you seek out your own happiness? You still have your free-dom. Your magick lies within you. It is more than many Fae would be left with. Is there any chance you can create a life you love within your circumstances?"

"I don't know," Rian surprised her by answering. His hand tightened around hers. "I haven't tried. I've been so focused on seeking my revenge that all I can see is that path. It's given me purpose."

"What a cold and distressing life it must be if only fueled by revenge."

"Yes, well, sometimes choices are taken from us," Rian gritted out.

"Some, yes. But not all," Terra whispered, a yearning to ease his pain filling her. He had every right to feel the way he did, and yet she hoped he would be able to find a way forward that wasn't solely defined by his hatred. At some point, wasn't it exhausting to live in bitterness?

"No. Not all." Rian seemed to catch her meaning, and he did something that not only surprised Terra, but seemed to surprise himself as well. Putting their glasses aside, Rian pulled Terra into his lap and cradled her.

Oh, but this man needed a hug, Terra realized.

Shifting in his lap so she could see his face, she wrapped her arms around his chest and watched a tangle of emotions twist across his handsome features. His eyes were shuttered, and his breath hitched, as though the internal struggle pained him.

Once more, Terra let silence do the work. There were some wounds that words couldn't heal. But maybe, just maybe, togetherness could. She held tight, matching her breath to his, and their bodies melded together, their energy blending. In her hug was an apology for her people, and in his was grief. As the moment drew out, Terra sensed a shift.

Imperceptible at first, but then warmth bloomed beneath where his hand had begun to idly stroke her back. Fire raced beneath his fingertips as he ran them from her tailbone all the way up to her shoulders and back again, finding the dips and curves of her back. She wanted to arch into his hand and purr like a cat, so hypnotic was his touch. As desire built in her core, Terra shifted on his lap, a soft sigh of contentment escaping as his other hand massaged her side. Still, he didn't look at her, and she drank in his visage unimpeded while his hands wandered her body of their own accord. It was as though once he'd started touching, he was helpless to stop, and Terra realized that now his internal struggle had nothing to do with his grief.

Instead, he was trying to resist her.

Her suspicions were confirmed when she reached out and traced a finger across his jawline. Immediately, Rian stiffened at her touch and then turned and caught her index finger with his lips. He brushed a kiss over her skin before taking her finger into his mouth.

Wet, sensual, heat.

Rian sucked gently, before surprising her with a quick scrape of his teeth. Liquid heat filled her, and the ocean-soaked breeze seemed cooler now against her flushed skin. Terra found herself shifting on his lap, her need for him building, and he bent his head forward to nuzzle into her neck. Still he couldn't look at her, Terra realized. She started when he blew a hot breath against her skin, her nipples puckering at the sensation, his hands massaging her body through the silk of her dress.

She'd always loved the feeling of silk on her skin, but now with his hands massaging her body so expertly? Silk might be her undoing. No longer caring about keeping walls up, Terra dropped her head back and arched her breasts toward him. An offering.

A demand.

His chuckle at her throat would have irritated her if he had ignored her needs but, instead, he cupped a breast with one hand, trailing his finger over the perked bud of her nipple, the softness of his touch through the silk of her dress sending shivers across her body. She squirmed once more in his lap, letting out a helpless mewling sound, his breath hot at her neck as he massaged her breasts.

"A body made for my touch," Rian said. "It's a goddess you are, Terra. Since the moment I saw you, I wanted my hands on you."

"I ... is that ... right?" Terra gasped, her eyes fluttering closed as he slid his hands across the silk in soft circular motions, her breasts growing warm at his touch. She needed him. Desperately so. The fated mate bond was singing in her heart, and she was tempted to sing their heartsong.

To claim him.

But not yet, Terra reminded herself, trying to pull her mind from the delicious ecstasy he was wielding on her body. They needed more time.

He needed more time.

"Open for me, darling," Rian said at her throat. One hand was still wrapped around her waist, steadying her on his lap, while his other now inched its way up her calf. "Let me return the pleasure you showed me last night."

Was that all this was? Evening the score? If so, Terra wasn't sure she wanted him to have the upper hand. And yet, her legs widened, as though she had no control over them, and she buried her face in the hard muscles of his chest as his fingertips danced across the soft flesh of her thigh. There he lingered, matching the stroke of her thigh with that at her waist, and Terra's tension eased under his rhythmic touch. Only when she relaxed in his arms, did he finally ease higher to trace a hand lightly over where she wanted him most.

Terra was aching for his touch and, when he parted her, sliding his finger into her wet heat, she convulsed around his hand. It shocked her, this response to him, and she kept her face at his chest as pleasure rocketed through her body and her cheeks flamed.

"A beautiful Goddess you are. Just look at you taking pleasure from my touch. We've only just begun, haven't we?" Rian's hand continued to stroke her, and desire built in her core once more, and she felt both trapped and free, locked against his muscular body, as he patiently and expertly brought her to the edge once more and tossed her over with fearless abandon.

"Rian," Terra panted, throwing her head back as waves of pleasure washed over her body. "You ... I ... want to give you the same."

"No." Rian withdrew his hand and shifted her so that their faces met. "Don't you understand, Terra? This *is* my pleasure."

With that, he claimed her lips in the softest of kisses, and cradled her like she was a snow globe that would shatter if he dropped her. Nobody had taken such care with her before, Terra realized. She was so used to being in charge, and nurturing everyone else, that she had never allowed someone else to attend to her. Now, as Rian kissed her like she was the most delicate gift in the world, her heart cracked open, and love spilled out.

THE TWO DOMNUA watched the lovers from afar, hidden behind a rocky outcrop of boulders. They'd been sent to find Rian and get an update on where he stood with the mission that their Goddess had assigned to him.

"He chooses her." The Dark Fae shifted, turning away.

"Goddess Domnu must be told."

"We'll go at once."

Together, the two slipped into the darkness.

13

ANOTHER RESTLESS NIGHT, sleep only coming to him finally when he drank the tea that Terra had made for him, and still Rian woke at the first brush of morning light. Nurturer, he thought, with a small smile. There was something about Terra that eased some of the perpetual tension that had plagued him for years now. He thought of her now, as he stood at his doorway and watched the sun kiss the sky. Would she sleep easily after the pleasure he'd given her last night? Or had he given her the same mixture of confused emotions as he now carried?

She *should* hate him for stealing the amulet.

Instead, she had healed his wounds, brewed him tea, and allowed him the gift of touching her miraculous body. How could a person be so endlessly patient and forgiving? It almost didn't seem real to him. Forgiveness was not a notion that Rian had made friends with.

She'd fought for him.

There was no possibility that she was lying to him about her actions after he'd been exiled. The sadness in her eyes when she spoke of the estrangement with her family mirrored his own. Like recognized like, Rian realized. And here was a woman who endured grief because she stood for what she believed to be the truth. She'd never even met him, and yet a single look from him had been enough for her to try and reverse his judgment. Even if her actions had been too late, the fact was — she'd tried. Nobody else had cared. His mother's pleas for help had fallen on deaf ears. His friends from that life had abandoned him, siding with the High Council instead. But Terra? A woman he'd never met had stood for him.

And now he'd stolen her amulet.

It was a very concerning thing, feeling his emotions again, Rian realized as he rubbed at an ache that bloomed in his chest. Life had been much easier when he could ice everything out and drown his grief in anger and egregious amounts of whiskey. He never should have agreed with Goddess Domnu's plan—not that he'd had all that much say in it. She'd more or less ordered him to set out on this path, but it wasn't like he'd put up much of a fight. Not when she dangled the promise of discovering the identity of the man responsible for his fate at his fingertips. Rian's hands clenched around his mug, and he worked to steady his breathing before he accidently let his magick loose and destroyed the very cliffs their cottages were perched upon. He was too keyed up to stay inside, and though the wind that raced across the meadow carried with it the promise of rain, Rian grabbed his jacket and left his cottage. He needed to put space between him and Terra because the image of her waking up, her skin soft in the misty morning light, was enough to make him almost rabid for her touch. Veering sharply away from the cottages, he stumbled down a narrow path that wound him toward a tiny beach, fervently praying for an answer to his conundrum.

He reached the water just as a light rain began to fall, and, tilting his face up to the sky, he welcomed the cold stab of raindrops on his face. Maybe the rain would numb him once more, and he wouldn't be worried about hurting someone else. Had any of the Earth Fae cared about hurting him? Or how his mother felt — dying alone with nobody around her?

"Foolish."

At the hiss beside him, Rian whirled, his dagger already in his hand. A group of Domnua surrounded him, a faint silver glow hovering around their bodies, their eyes all but dead inside. Rian caught a flash of light just below the surface of the water that now roiled tumul-tuously to the sand.

"I'm foolish? Why's that, friends?" Rian said, rocking back and forth lightly on his heels, ready for a fight. Make no mistake about it, the Domnua were nobody's friends.

"Friend? Or foe? Which is it, outcast?" What seemed to be the lead Domnua stepped forward, his ugly visage twisted in disgust.

"I'm no foe to you. However, I can't promise your safety if you threaten me." Rian shrugged, acting nonchalant. His heart rate picked up as he realized that if the Domnua had found him here, they likely had found Terra as well. The camp had been well asleep when he'd left, which meant an ambush from the Domnua could kill them all. Fear clouded his vision, and he had to force himself not to turn his back on the threat in front of him and race back to where Terra slept.

"We come to find where your loyalties lie." The words came out almost like a hiss, reminding Rian of Goddess Domnu's mane of serpent hair.

"My loyalties have nothing to do with my agreement with the Goddess. I never pledged allegiance to your people, I'll remind you of that," Rian said.

"You'd make a promise and betray it in the same breath?"

"You're hardly one to speak of broken promises. I well know your people's history of trying to win by any costs necessary. Don't come crying to me about betrayals and holding onto vows when you've built your kingdom on broken promises. You'll kill a man as he's promising fealty as easily as you'll lie and tell me the Goddess has my back. For the record — you're as expendable to her as I am. Make no mistake that her highness considers you disposable." Rian didn't care if he angered the Dark Fae. He'd rather provoke them into a reaction that warranted him killing them all so he could return quickly to the camp than sit here and trade threats and half-truths all morning.

"It's an honor to die for our Goddess." The leader bowed his head but raised his sword. Rian's words had worked. As one, the group descended upon him, and he leaped into the fray, his blood humming with the anticipation of battle, his magick at the ready. Here was an outlet for his fury, here he could let loose the violence that simmered beneath the surface. He took great joy in sending his dagger through the eye of the leader, his ugly face freezing in pain and disbelief, before disintegrating in an explosion of silvery blood. Rocketing forward, Rian scooped up his knife, and whirled to kick the legs of another Fae out beneath him. As the Fae tumbled, Rian caught the blade across his throat, ending his life instantly. He'd be lying if he said it wasn't fulfilling to see the Dark Fae explode at his hands, but he had no time to linger in his accomplishments as pain sliced his shoulder.

"Wrong choice, boyo." Rian reached up and ripped the blade from his shoulder, wincing as the knife tore at his flesh. Likely poisoned, the blade was, and he'd need Callahan's help to heal that wound. If his friend still lived. The thought of the camp being under a similar siege sent a fresh wave of rage through him, and Rian made quick work of the remaining Domnua, through magick and simple force of will. When the last had exploded, leaving the small beach covered in silvery traces of blood, Rian turned to race back.

"Brother."

Whirling, Rian gaped at a Water Fae that had surfaced.

"Do you need our assistance?"

"I'm an outcast. Exiled. You'd still help me?" Right, so he definitely still had a chip on his shoulder. Speaking of shoulders, dark magick worked its way through his muscles, and he knew he needed to act soon.

"Yes. We'd help you. You fight on the side of good," the Water Fae explained, as though it was as simple as that. And maybe it was. As much as he wanted to resist the offer of help, he had other people to think about.

"The Domnua will likely attack here. I'll accept any offer of help you can bring."

"It is done."

Rian didn't wait for more. Instead, he raced up the narrow path toward the cottages, the dark magick of the Domnua making his gait awkward and stilted. Still, fear drove him forward, and, as he crested the last hill, he almost stumbled at what he saw.

Terra stood, covered in silver blood, and called for him.

"Terra." Her name was but a whisper at his lips, and he understood how quickly the Dark Fae's magick was weakening him. And yet ... she heard. Turning, her eyes widened, and she screeched his name as Rian dropped to his knees.

"Rian. No, Rian. What's happened. Where?" Terra gasped, kneeling at his side and wrapping her arms around him. "Please, love. Tell *me*. Where are you hurt? I need to see it. I can help you. Callahan!" Terra turned her head and screamed for his friend, relieving his other fear that the old man had been hurt.

Love. His heart twisted at that word, hopeful and uncertain, like a new doe finding its feet.

"Knife to my back. Shoulder." Rian turned to show his back to Terra, and her quick intake of breath was all he needed to know that it was bad.

"Sure and I can't leave you alone for two seconds now, can I?" Callahan's cheerful voice sounded at his ear, and Rian closed his eyes in relief. His friend was safe. Their voices blurred together as they conferred over his wound, and he just stayed, kneeling in the rain, conserving his energy. He focused on the thread of magick that wound through him, imagining it fighting off the Dark Fae's poison.

Several hands pressed to his shoulder, and Rian winced as the iciness increased, as though it wanted to resist being pulled from him. This pain didn't numb, no, the dark magick burned, and he gasped for breath as they pulled the spell from his shoulder while chanting over him. Dots danced before his eyelids, and Rian focused on schooling his breath, trying his best to not embarrass himself by passing out on the spot.

At once, as though someone had pulled a thorn from his foot, the pain receded, and the muscles of his shoulder carefully knit back together.

"There now, that should be better, right?" Terra asked, crouching by his side. She pressed her hand to his brow, and he was so grateful to see her unharmed that he turned and pressed a kiss to her palm, not caring if the others saw. They already knew he'd taken her on a date, didn't they? It wasn't like he needed to hide his attraction for her.

It was more than attraction.

Rian pushed that thought quickly aside, uncomfortable with this new territory that his heart seemed more than delighted to dance into.

"Come on, boyo. Let's get you out of the mud." Callahan hooked an arm under Rian's and helped ease him to standing. Once there, Rian took a moment to steady himself, and was happy to find that other than a few twinges when he rolled his shoulder, everything had healed nicely. A thought occurred to him, and he narrowed his eyes at Callahan.

"Did you take the pain in?" Rian referred to the ancient process of healing wherein the caretaker would draw the sickness out with their hands. If the illness wasn't directed appropriately, the healer would bear the brunt of the pain.

"Not me." Callahan nodded to where Bianca had an arm wrapped around Terra.

"Please tell me you didn't..." Rian grabbed Terra's hands, searching her face.

"No, no. I let it wash through me, but the Earth took it. I'm okay. It just gave me a small fright is all. Are you well then?" Terra's soulful eyes searched his, and a thousand words jammed themselves into his head at once as he tried to articulate his thoughts. He wanted...

"Well, now, isn't this interesting?" A venomous voice sounded from behind them, and Rian whirled, placing himself in front of Terra to shield her. Goddess Domnu stood in the meadow, the rain disappearing so as not to irritate her serpents and smiled brightly at Rian. "Making friends, are we, Rian?"

"One of yours attacked me," Rian said, diverting the conversation away from Terra.

"Ah, yes, unfortunate, wasn't that? I see you've survived nicely though." Goddess Domnu's eyes sharpened as Terra stepped out from behind Rian, and dread filled him. Why couldn't she just stay behind him where he could protect her? "You've been quite expedient in acquiring what we agreed upon. The amulet?" Goddess Domnu held out her hand, steady in her assurance that

Rian would follow her command. Madness twirled behind her eyes, and a shiver of fear trickled through Rian.

"It isn't his to give," Terra said, lifting her chin at the Goddess.

Her expression sharpened before she threw back her head and laughed, the snakes mimicking her as they danced around her head.

"Silly fool. You think your power matches mine? Don't you know that I *always* get what I want?"

"Actually ... that's not quite true, is it?" Bianca piped up from the other side of him, and Rian caught Seamus's whispered curse on the wind. Bloody hell, but these women were impervious to danger. "I seem to remember you desperately wanting the Four Treasures ... and yet, we managed to keep those out of your nasty little hands, didn't we?"

"Bianca," Rian warned. Did she have any idea the power that Goddess Domnu held?

"Ah yes, I remember you. Annoying human, I'm surprised you're still around." Goddess Domnu glared at Bianca.

"I'm stubborn like that."

Shockingly, Goddess Domnu laughed once more. "You're amusing, I'll admit. I'll let you live. This time. Be careful though... I may not be in this good a mood next time I see you."

Seamus clamped a hand over Bianca's mouth before she could retort, and Rian couldn't blame the man, though he was certain Bianca must have bitten his palm when he swore once more and hissed in his wife's ear.

"The amulet?" Goddess Domnu looked to Rian.

"As I said, it's not his to give," Terra repeated.

"We had a deal, outcast." Domnu leveled Rian with a look.

"There's ... a few complications." Rian stalled, unsure of how to proceed. What he did know was that he couldn't give up the knife yet, at the same time, he had brokered a deal with the Goddess. Perhaps if he told her that he no longer sought revenge on the man who was responsible for his exile? If so, he could release her from her end of the bargain and he wouldn't owe her anything. He opened his mouth to say as much when she lifted a hand to stop him from speaking.

"I kept *my* end of the pact. You're indebted to me now. Think long and hard about what you plan to do with the knife because the next time I return, I will only ask once for the amulet." Goddess Domnu waved her hand and a man appeared out of thin air, his wrists bound behind his back, blood weeping from a wound at his forehead. Domnu's grin widened, her eyes bright and interested, and she paused as she waited for Rian's reaction. "Here is the man who is responsible for your exile. The true betrayer. He is yours to kill."

Fury filled him, and Rian took an involuntary step toward the man, rage roaring its way through his body. He wanted nothing more than to destroy the man who knelt in front of him, his blood seeping into the Earth. Domnu smiled, her snakes slithering around her head, and crossed her arms to watch the show.

"You owe me, Rian." Domnu reminded him, her voice joyful.

"Cormac. *No*." The tremulous voice at his side had Rian whirling to where Terra stood, her face frozen in shock, her mouth gaping open.

Cormac? Rian's thoughts took a minute to catch up.

Oh. That Cormac.

This was Terra's younger brother.

Which meant ... dread filled him as he realized that the man he most wanted to destroy was the brother of the woman he'd most come to care for. Terra's mouth worked, but no sound came out, and he realized she was also processing her brother's lack of loyalty. What he wasn't expecting was for Terra to turn her burning gaze on him.

"You," Terra whispered. Jabbing a finger in the air at him, she advanced. "You did this. You knew it was Cormac, didn't you?"

"I didn't... Terra, I swear..." Rian held his hands up as she jabbed a finger into his chest in sharp little spikes.

"Well, now ... this is amusing, isn't it?" Goddess Domnu clapped her hands, like a child watching a puppet show, and almost danced in place as though she was having all the fun in the world.

"Away with you," Terra hissed, turning so fast that the Goddess didn't have time to react when Terra fired a wave of magick at her, pulling a shock of lightning from the sky to hit Domnu directly in the back. The Goddess stumbled forward, and Rian did all he could do in that moment — he joined Terra in attacking the Dark Goddess. Together, the group stepped forward, blasting Domnu with various magicks, until she winked from sight.

She wasn't dead, oh no, as that wasn't possible.

But she was gone for now.

"Terra." Rian stepped forward, but she held a hand up, refusing to look at him as she dropped to her knees in front of her younger brother.

"Oh, Cormac. How could you?" Terra breathed. Cormac looked up at her through the blood in his eyes and promptly fainted.

Terra caught him as he fell.

14

WHAT A FOOL SHE WAS.

Terra silently berated herself as she mopped the blood from Cormac's brow. Seamus and Callahan had carried him into Terra's cottage while Rian had given her one furious look and stormed away.

He was mad at *her*?

The gall of that man. If he thought for one moment that he would get to live out his revenge-seeking fantasy by killing her brother in front of her, he was going to learn just how powerful Terra really was. While she was furious with Cormac for the betrayal he'd wrought upon their brother — and their family — she also wasn't ready to let him die for a mistake he'd made.

Rian *must* have known. There was no way he could have asked after her family and then listened to her go on and on about her family estrangement, without having some idea that Cormac was the one responsible for Rian's exile. It was clear he'd made a pact with the Dark Fae, and the Goddess must have already had this knowledge.

Here she'd thought she'd been gaining some headway with Rian, and he'd been playing her all along. Fury at her blindness and stupidity filled her, not to mention shame for enjoying his touch so much last night. Had he been laughing at her the whole time? Silly Terra. Easy to manipulate and have his way with, all while keeping his end goal in sight.

"Terra?" Cormac's voice rasped, drawing her attention from her thoughts. Bianca hurried to his side with a glass of water, and he eyed the stranger curiously. "Where am I? What happened?"

"Oh, Cormac." Terra dropped onto the side of the bed and stared glumly at her younger brother. The cut on his forehead was deep, and it still wept openly, though they'd managed to stem the flow of blood a bit. Garish pink skin already turning to purple surrounded the wound, and his dark hair was matted with blood that had gone tacky. "What have you done?"

"Me? What do you mean?" Cormac's gaze danced everywhere, confirming Terra's suspicions.

"All this time..." Terra whispered, her heart breaking. He'd allowed her to become estranged from the family, handily sacrificing her in order to save his name. To protect his dirty little secret. Now, she was stuck in the position of having to protect her brother from her fated mate — who had an entirely valid reason for wanting to seek his revenge upon Cormac.

This, to put it mildly, was an absolute mess.

"Terra. Where are we? What's going on?" Cormac asked, continuing to look around the room. "Who is this?"

"Hi there. I'm Bianca, and it seems to me like you've landed yourself in some trouble here." Bianca offered him some more water.

"In trouble? Am *I* in trouble?" Cormac winced as he eased himself up a bit, bringing a hand to touch his forehead before Terra batted it away.

"Don't touch. We've only just stopped most of the bleeding."

"Blood? You'd better tell me what is going on. Right now." Cormac tried a serious tone, and Terra rolled her eyes. Like he was in any position to order her about?

"It was you. Wasn't it? With Marias?" At her words, Cormac stiffened and moved to get off the bed.

"I don't think so," Bianca said, holding a knife to his throat. Terra's eyes widened. "You'll be staying and answering your sister's questions."

"I ... I don't know what you're talking about." Cormac's gaze dropped to the left, and Terra's heart broke. Her own blood. He'd not only betrayed Eoghan, but he'd also lied to Terra and allowed her family to turn against her. The beloved brother she'd once known fell away, and now she stared at a man that she did not know.

"It's too late to lie, Cormac. The Goddess Domnu herself all but delivered you on a platter. Rian would be in his rights to seek his justice."

At Rian's name, Cormac's face paled.

"Terra ... you have to..." Cormac stuttered to a stop when she held up her hand to halt his words.

"No, Cormac. *I* don't have to do anything. You are a liar and a cheat. Imagine how Eoghan will react once he learns what you've done. You bring shame to our family, and yourself. We used to..." Terra's voice broke as tears filled her eyes. "We used to be best friends, me and you. It broke my heart when you both banded against me. But at least I could understand why. But this? No, Cormac. I can't understand this. Even if you never truly cared for me, you can't say you didn't love Eoghan."

"He always had to be perfect. Perfect life. Perfect job. Perfect wife." Cormac sneered, his mask dropping away, and Terra closed her eyes as her stomach twisted in pain. He might as well have put a knife to her gut, his words hurt that much. "And she *was* perfect. Perfect as a lover. Easy to seduce as well. I enjoyed her."

"Oh, Cormac. Why? To what end?" Terra begged of him, trying to understand what had driven his decision.

"I wanted to see a chink in Eoghan's armor. He never ... he never had time for me anymore. Not once he met her." Cormac's words were bitter, and Terra just shook her head. All of this heartbreak and lives ruined — because he was jealous that his big brother was giving attention to someone else. The sheer selfishness was astounding. It wasn't in Terra's nature to hate someone, but she realized she was dangerously close when her nails dug into her palms, and she lifted a fist at her brother. Seeing the expression on her face, Cormac flinched backwards.

"You pathetic baby of a man," Terra hissed. "You don't get what you want so you throw your toys out of the pram and destroy others' lives? Do you have any idea how selfish you are? If ... and this is a big if ... you get out of here alive, I will be bringing you before the High Council.

I do not care that you are my blood. Because all you are to me now is an embarrassment."

"Terra ... you wouldn't." Cormac gaped at her, clearly thinking that she would never expose him to Eoghan. "You can't tell Eoghan. You *can't*."

"Oh, I can. And I will. You've sowed your own seeds, Cormac. Now your lies will bear fruit."

"But ... Eoghan will ... he'll hate me." Cormac clutched her arm as she rose, and Terra wrenched herself free from his hand. His touch made her physically sick.

"Oh, it's Eoghan you're worried about, is it? Not the fact that you've managed to kick me out of the family and turn everyone against me? It's fine it is if I'm the one hurting, but not your precious Eoghan? You're a disgrace."

"I wouldn't say any more if I were you," Bianca advised him as Terra stormed for the door. "You've caused more problems than you can possibly know. Selfish little shite, aren't you? I'm guessing Terra's not wrong about calling you a big man baby."

"You can't speak to me..." Cormac trailed off, and Terra imagined that Bianca had a blade to his throat once more. She didn't worry for Bianca's safety, Cormac had never been strong with weapons or magick. In fact, he'd never been strong in any particular area other than charming people. Fury drove her into the pelting rain, and she stood for a moment, letting the cold drops wash across her skin, wishing for a way to make this all go away.

It was never that easy though, was it?

The earth rumbled beneath her feet, responding to her anger, and she realized she was furious. It was such an unusual emotion for the ever-patient Terra to feel, that she paced in a circle, enjoying the roar of the waves below the cliffs as they slammed into the rocks. She was *mad*. Mad at Cormac. Mad at her lost time with family. Mad that Rian had been exiled. Mad that Rian had used her emotions to get her brother here. At the last thought, Terra turned. At least she'd have a stronger opponent to direct her wrath at. Catching a glimpse of movement out of the corner of her eye, Terra watched Rian stomp his way toward the Cathedral Cliffs.

Well, you know what? She could stomp too.

Decided, Terra followed him, bringing each foot down so heavily that the earth shook with her steps, and she laughed with the power of her rage. The rain whipped around her head, as gale force winds gathered, and zeroed in on her prey as Rian skidded to a stop and turned. Like a banshee, Terra all but screamed her way to where he stood, swinging wildly between laughter and rage, only coming to a stop when Rian brandished a knife at her.

"Back off," Rian hissed.

"Me? Oh now he's wanting me to back off, is it?" Terra threw her head back and laughed, the icy rain pelting her face, and she was beginning to think she was becoming a touch unhinged. "You weren't saying that last night when you had your hands all over me, were you? Or the night before when I brought you to completion? Now it's *me* backing off that you're wanting?"

"The edge is close. I won't have your rage tossing me off the side to be speared on those rocks below," Rian shouted as the wind picked up, pushing him back. "Call off your wind. Have you lost your damn mind?"

Terra had to forcibly remind herself of what Rian had also lost at the hands of her own brother and focused on schooling her breath until the winds that threatened to push them both over the edge eased off. Far below them, the ocean raged, slamming repeatedly into the sharp pillars of rock that jutted to the sky.

"You knew. Didn't you? You'd made that pact with Domnu ... and you knew. That ... that..." Terra had to push the words out. Her entire body was shivering now, with anger, and sadness, as she tried to wrap her head around two different men she cared for betraying her.

"That's what you're in a fuss about?" Rian's laugh was bitter. "You're mad because you think that I knew about your brother? Sorry, princess. I had no idea your brother was the one I could thank for my extended vacation to the human realm. But I look forward to thanking him. In great and painstaking detail."

"You can't..." Terra stopped and pressed her fingers to her eyes. Her heart thudded in her chest as worry for her brother twisted low in her stomach. She couldn't just turn off and on her love for Cormac, even though he apparently could do the same for her. Her brother deserved his punishment, of that she was certain, but not like this.

"Oh ... but I can. Don't you see? You don't rule here, princess. I'm the one who's in control. We're not in your realm anymore, are we?" Rian bent forward so his face was inches from hers, and she could read the fury and confusion that warred in his eyes.

"What are you going to do with him?" Terra was furious with herself for caring, but still she felt like she had to look out for her little brother.

"I don't know yet, Terra. I need a moment to consider my most painful options."

"I thought... I thought I meant something to you..."

"What does this have to do with you?" Rian stepped away from the edge of the cliffs, advancing so fast that Terra had to take three steps backward for every one of his. When he'd pushed her sufficiently away from the edge, he grasped her wrists. His touch still warmed her, though she was furious that her body responded to him at all. "Unless you knew your brother committed this crime?"

"I didn't... I swear it." How could he even think that of her? Tears pricked her eyes, and confusion warred inside of her. She didn't know who to be mad at anymore. She just knew that she had all this anger bubbling inside of her, and there was no place for it to go. It was like a teakettle with no steam valve to release the pressure.

"And neither did I, princess. It was just as big a shock to me that your darling brother was responsible for me missing out on my mother's final days as it was to you then. So don't come spewing your rage at me, darling. It's misdirecting your pain, you are."

At that, Terra really looked at Rian. Well and truly looked at him. Rain dripped down the craggy edges of his handsome face, though his eyes burned brightly, ravaged with emotion. He held her in one spot, his hands tight at her wrists, his touch burning her skin.

She had a choice to make. She could believe he'd

deliberately lied to her and used the secret of her brother's betrayal as a way to manipulate and destroy everything on his path to revenge, or she could take a leap of faith that Rian truly hadn't known about Cormac's actions. It was easier, in some respects, to be angry, wasn't it? From a vaguely objective viewpoint, Terra could understand why Rian had held onto this emotion all these years. Anger was more comfortable than vulnerability.

So she did what her heart begged her to do.

Terra chose to believe her fated mate.

Meeting his gaze, she dug deep and sang their heartsong.

15

THE SONG THUNDERED THROUGH RIAN, riveting him to the spot.

Already he was confused about how to move forward now that the thing he wanted most had been delivered, quite literally, at his feet. But this?

This was too much.

Terra was his fated mate.

She'd known, all along, that they were fated. And yet had said nothing. No wonder he'd been so pulled to her since the moment he saw her. Everything lined up in sudden and stunning clarity.

The nice gestures, the kisses, the healing of his wounds — she'd been playing him all along. On top of it, she'd had the nerve to storm out onto these cliffs and accuse him of misleading her? Fury blinded him, and he dropped her wrists before he did something stupid like heave her over the edge of the cliff.

Of course, he couldn't do that. Their connection would make it impossible for him to truly hurt her. But still. He was sorely tempted to be done with her, and all of this, and just transport himself to another time and place where he could nurse his wounds in private. Unfortunately, if he left now, Goddess Domnu would surely return and use her favorite scorched-earth technique on the island.

When the song finished, Terra stood before him, glorious in her ferocity, her chest heaving as the wind whipped her hair around her head. She waited, her lips parted, and he'd never wanted anyone more than in this moment. Grabbing the back of her head, Rian threaded his fingers through her sodden hair and crushed his mouth to hers, feasting on what was his.

She was *his*.

And he had no idea what to do about it. The very thought that he could have a lifetime of touching Terra, waking next to Terra, going to bed with Terra was both exhilarating and terrifying. Anger had been his bedmate for so long, he wasn't sure he even knew how to be a partner to someone. Terra moaned into his mouth, and Rian drank in the sweetness of her kiss as he let his hands roam her body. Strength and softness, fury and love, Terra was everything.

And he'd made a deal with the devil.

It took everything in his power to break the kiss and to step back, back, back until he stood in the middle of the soggy meadow, a sullen gray mist surrounding him. As much as his body begged for him to bury himself deep inside Terra, to lose himself to the rush of desire that raged inside of him, he couldn't do it. Not here. Not like this.

It was too complicated, everything that just happened, and, if he claimed Terra now, he'd no longer be making decisions on his own. No, once a claim was made, choices had to be made between two people. Compromises, even. The last time someone had made a choice for him was when he'd been exiled. Rian refused to let someone else have that kind of power over him again. Even if it meant turning his back on his fated mate.

Even when his mate was as glorious as Terra.

It was all too much, too confusing, and, after years of freezing out his emotions, they all seemed to arise at once, threatening to overwhelm and engulf him much like the waves that crashed far below. So, for once, he was going to take Callahan's advice and wait. Without another word, he turned and left Terra standing in the rain, her face ravaged with sorrow. Maybe the decision he made now wouldn't be forever, but it would have to be for now. At least until he got his head on straight. The ground rumbled beneath his feet, and he rolled his eyes, not caring that the Earth was unhappy with him.

Rian needed an outlet for his emotions, and he had just the ticket.

The wind whipped up once more, and he struggled against it, as though Terra herself commanded him back to her. Rian pushed out with his magick, pressing back against the wind, as he strode across the uneven terrain until the cottages came into view among the mist. Callahan stood in front of Terra's cottage, his arms crossed, rain dripping from the brim of the hat he'd pulled low on his forehead.

"Is he in there?" Rian asked, stopping short when Callahan blocked his way.

"What did you do with Lady Terra?" Callahan lifted his chin at him, and Rian realized that Terra had somehow gained Callahan's loyalty too. Was there anyone she didn't enchant? He'd watched birds swoop down and land on her shoulder, insects wander her way, and he wouldn't be surprised if all the animals in the forest followed her in a parade. There wasn't much not to love. Except for her dishonesty, he reminded himself. She'd concealed from him their bond. How had she even learned of it? Perhaps rulers were given this knowledge far before the regular Fae were.

Except ... he'd been the first one to sing their song, hadn't he? One drunken evening, wandering home, it had just burst out of him like some inspired poetry, and a homeless drunk on the corner had joined him in song. After that, the song had escaped him periodically, only on the severe edges of fatigue or drunkenness, and he vaguely could remember perhaps hearing it in a dream. So had it been him who initiated their bond? Rian shook his head, as though he could physically clear the thoughts from his brain, and refocused on Callahan.

"I left her up on the ridge. Unharmed."

"Rian..."

"Don't." Rian shouldered Callahan aside and slammed the door to Terra's cottage open, causing Bianca to jump. Seamus straightened from where he stood against the wall, a sour expression on his face.

"Rian. Where's Terra?" Bianca ran to him, surprising

him by putting her arms around him in a hug. A *hug*. Why was this woman, his captive, hugging him?

An even bigger question was — why did he want to lean into it? There was something so mothering and soothing about Bianca's charms that he almost found himself bowing into her arms to receive the care she sought to give him. But when he caught sight of Cormac over Bianca's shoulder, his resolve tightened. Gently, he removed Bianca's arms from around him and nudged her backwards, fully knowing that Seamus would have his head if he did anything to upset Bianca. While a good fight with Seamus might ease some of this anger he carried, that wasn't a battle he'd be choosing. He'd seen it well enough himself over the years. Love was a powerful foe.

"Terra's just fine. She's up on the ridge, howling about this or that. She's not my concern at the moment. This one is." Rian stood over Cormac and looked down at the man who had taken his last moments with his mother away from him. "Leave me."

"I don't think that's a good idea," Seamus said.

"Leave!" Rian forced a wave of magick at the both of them, causing them to be pushed toward the door, and, though they struggled to fight it, he was too strong for them. Once he'd seen them through the door, Rian snapped his fingers and slammed it shut, putting up an invisible shield so nobody could interrupt him.

He could see Terra in Cormac's features. They shared the same golden-green eyes and proud tilt to their heads. The similarities ended there, however. Where warmth bloomed in Terra's gaze, here Rian found a languid nonchalance in Cormac's. Did the man have any idea just how much trouble he was in? Or did he even care? He should be cowering in fear, and instead his lip curled in a sneer as he looked up at Rian. When he made a move to stand from the bed, Rian slapped him directly across the face, knocking him back onto the mattress.

"Ouch!" Cormac gasped, bringing a hand to his face.

Rian smiled.

He could have punched the man, or delivered a much more serious blow, but he kind of enjoyed insulting him with a slap. There was time enough for him to seek his vengeance on Cormac. For now, maybe he'd play a bit — like a cat taunting a mouse before it finally pounced.

"Oh, poor thing. Did I hurt you?" Rian all but purred, hoping Cormac would try and make a run for it again. When he did, predictably so, Rian gave him a tiny lead before launching himself across the cottage and tackling the man onto the rough planks of the wood floor. Sure, he could have used magick to stop Cormac from escaping, but, right now, it was physical violence he was craving. He happily pummeled Cormac in the ribs, twisting as the man kicked back, trying to nail him between the legs.

"Oh, now, that's not a fair fight, is it?" Rian asked, pinning one of Cormac's arms behind his back and slamming his forehead into the floor. Rian was rewarded with a delightful spray of blood when the wound from earlier reopened. Oh yes, this *was* satisfying. Perhaps he lingered too long in his amusement, because Cormac managed to catch him unawares, snapping his head back and butting Rian in the face. At the sharp taste of blood at his lips, Rian smiled again.

"Tsk, tsk, wee man. You'll not win this fight, but I'm more than happy to go a round or two with you."

"Then stand and fight me like a man," Cormac challenged. Rian laughed, his blood warming to the violence, before bringing his lips close to Cormac's ears.

"Like a man, you say? You mean like when you betrayed your own brother? With his fated mate? Is that what a man does?"

"Feck off," Cormac gasped, increasing his squirming beneath Rian's grip.

"Or was it when you laid with his wife? Was that you being a man?"

"At least I could bring her to pleasure. Unlike him," Cormac said, and Rian shook his head.

"I find that hard to believe. It's sort of a given that fated mates can pleasure each other. What did it take, Cormac, to convince Marias to betray her mate? What did you hold over her?" Rian realized he was right in his line of questioning when Cormac stilled beneath him. So. Perhaps Eoghan's wife hadn't fully betrayed him, but instead had been blackmailed into doing so. Interesting.

And yet ... not. It didn't change the outcome of matters, did it? He'd still taken the fall for this whiny piece of crap masquerading as a man. When Cormac whipped his head to the side, trying to bite Rian's face, he leaned back. Hauling the man up, Rian shoved him so that he stumbled across the room, tripping on the bench and barely catching himself before he faceplanted on the wall. Cormac turned, blood dripping down his face once more, the light of battle in his eyes.

"Well? It's just you and me here, Cormac. Do you even

know who I am?" It suddenly occurred to Rian that Cormac might not even be aware of the man who had been judged in his place. At the very least, he should introduce Cormac to the man who now determined his future.

"Aye, I do." Cormac steadied himself, wiping blood from his eyes with the back of his hand. "You're Rian. Head of Magicks. Outcast."

"Oh see, for a moment there I was thinking to go easy on you. But you make it quite hard to be nice." Rian pressed his lips together, the coppery tang of his own blood fueling the fight inside of him. "You might as well tell me Cormac. You're going to die either way."

Rian blocked the first paltry wave of magick that Cormac tossed at him, a spear of ice, as easily as if a child had come up to him and kicked him in the shin. His grin widened.

"Is that fighting like a man? I thought you wanted to give it a go. Come on then. I'll even let you go first." Rian offered his chin, waiting for the man to land a blow. Cormac rocked back and forth on his feet, his hands in the air, before leaping at Rian and landing an uppercut to his chin. The blow snapped Rian's head back, the pain validating all of his emotions, and his arms were already coming up to block Cormac's next punches. The man could throw a punch, Rian had to concede, but sheer force didn't make up for lack of style. With one twist, Rian kicked Cormac's knee out, and snapped his head back with a nasty straight cross as he fell to the floor again. There, he curled for a moment, wheezing, and Rian happily kicked him in the ribs.

"Shite," Cormac wheezed, doubling over, coughing. Blood splattered from his mouth to the floor once more and Rian chuckled, enjoying this much more than he thought he would have. He'd put all of his other emotions neatly back in a box, and only allowed anger to fuel his current mission.

"Speak, Cormac. Now's the time."

"Eoghan couldn't get Marias pregnant. They'd been trying for a long time. So I stepped in to do what he couldn't. I suggested it, and she took me up on it. I didn't blackmail her, and it was easy enough to seduce her. The promise of my strong seed? How could she resist? She liked it, too. I know that, once I was with her, she could tell what a better lover than Eoghan I was. She kept coming back to me, didn't she?"

"I wouldn't know." Rian slammed his fist into Cormac's face again, simply to watch the blood spray across the floor once more. "And what about your sister?"

"What about her?" Cormac wheezed, scuttling away on all fours when Rian eased off of him. He let the man crawl to the other side of the room and then pull himself up on the bed frame.

"What about her? You fought with her, didn't you? Your entire family stopped speaking to her. Because she dared to ask questions."

"Stupid. She should have left well enough alone. It's her own fault, isn't it? Asking too many questions. Taking care of your mother. She should have let it be—"

Cormac gasped as Rian was upon him, pinning him to the wall by his throat. His eyes bulged as he gasped for air.

"What did you say about my mother?" Rian's voice was deadly calm, and he squeezed tighter, enjoying the way panic skittered through Cormac's eyes.

"She... Terra ... took care of..."

"Rian! No!" Terra shrieked from behind him. Only she was strong enough to break his shield, Rian realized, as her hands came around his waist and pulled at him. Still he held on, wanting to take Cormac's last breath from him, much like he'd stolen Rian's last moments with his mother. "Stop, please stop. It's not worth it. Please, please... I'll take him to High Council. We'll have him punished. Please, Rian. You can't have this on your conscience."

She wept, Rian realized. Not for Cormac. But for him.

Slowly, Rian released his grip on Cormac, and the man crumpled to a ball on the floor.

"You stand for him. Even when he betrayed you. You're as much a victim at his hands as I am." Rian spoke to the wall, where streaks of Cormac's blood were smeared into the wood. Terra's arms were still wrapped around him from behind, and he could feel the soft press of her breasts heaving against his back as she sobbed.

"I fight for peace, Rian. I only want peace. And justice. Violence does nothing."

"I don't know about that. I feel pretty good right now." Rian looked down at her hands, so very tiny, clenched at his waist. Gently, he untangled himself from her grip and stepped back before turning to look down at Terra.

"Oh, Rian. Your face." Terra moved forward, her hand raised, but he stepped back. His adrenaline was too high from fighting with Cormac, as well as the information he'd gleaned from the man. He didn't know whether he'd hurt Terra or throw her to the ground and take her over and over until she screamed his name. Either way, he couldn't be touched right now.

"Is it true? My mother? You cared for her?" Rian clenched his fists at his side, his future hanging on Terra's next words.

"I ... well, I did what I could for her, Rian. She didn't have many people after you were exiled..." Terra trailed off when Rian winced.

"And?" Rian asked. He needed to know. Terra was now the last link he had to his mother — the last person potentially to have ever spoken to her.

"She was a lovely woman, Rian. She loved you so very much." Terra's eyes were bright with tears as she watched him. Even now, when he'd walked away from her on the cliffs, she'd come back and saved him. Ever the nurturer, his Terra. She was too good for him, too good for her family, and he was no match for her. What kind of man was he —one who sought vengeance and the destruction of the Earth Fae — to be a mate to someone so pure?

"Were you with her ... when she died?" Rian's voice came out in a rasp.

"I was, Rian. She went peacefully if it helps you to know it. I planted a bush for her, after ... with a small ceremony. By my favorite spot at the stream."

Of course she had, Rian thought. Because that's the kind of woman Terra was. His heart broke open, knowing that his mother hadn't suffered alone like he'd thought all these years.

"Thank you."

It was all Rian could say before he forced himself to walk away from the cottage before the grief that he'd done such a good job of hiding all these years over-whelmed him and he killed Terra's brother in front of her. At the moment, him leaving was the kindest thing he could do for her.

"Alright then, lad. Let's walk it off, eh?" Seamus met him at the door and swung an arm over his shoulders.

Rian didn't look back.

16

"Are you going to heal him?" The mattress dipped as Bianca eased down next to where Terra sat, staring glumly at her bloodied brother.

"I don't know," Terra admitted. Once Rian had left the cottage, Cormac had closed his eyes and succumbed to his pain, sliding into unconsciousness. His breathing came evenly, so Terra wasn't immediately worried for his safety, though she still hated seeing him this way.

Silly, she supposed. Cormac hadn't cared about hurting her, had he? Instead, he'd done whatever he'd wanted, happy to ruin other people's lives, so long as he came out smelling like roses.

"You don't have to, you know. Sometimes..." Bianca trailed off and tapped a finger against her lips.

"Sometimes what?" Terra tilted her head to look at Bianca. A streak of dirt smudged her face, and her blonde hair stuck out in frizzy tufts around her head.

"Well, you know... you reap what you sow and all that. It sounds like your brother had this coming to him.

Maybe it's a good thing that he feels this pain? It might help him to learn and not make similar mistakes in the future. Pain can be a powerful teacher."

"It can be." Terra was reminded of the time she'd seen a young rabbit frolicking in the fields, dancing dangerously close to the edge of the river. In seconds, the young animal had toppled over the embankment and into the icy water. By the time she'd reached the river, the rabbit had managed to make it to the embankment and had pulled itself, shivering and soaked, onto the sun-warmed dirt. It had lain there for quite a while, stunned and shivering in the midday sun, and Terra had wanted to ease its suffering. But she'd stopped herself, knowing the rabbit would learn a lesson, and that sometimes it was best not to interfere with nature.

Cormac reminded her a bit of that rabbit, huddled in shock, curled in on himself. Except it hadn't been a mistake that had almost killed him, it had been his own actions. Maybe the hardest thing to learn when you loved someone was that you couldn't always protect them from themselves.

"How are you feeling? What happened when you went after Rian?" Bianca asked, bumping her shoulder against Terra's. A bone-deep exhaustion washed through Terra, and all she wanted to do was curl up and sleep for days and pretend none of this had happened. She couldn't decide what was worse — having her fated mate turn his back on her or learning her brother had betrayed their entire family. Frankly, both made her miserable.

"I got mad at him. He yelled at me. I showed him I

was his fated mate. He rejected me," Terra summed it up as quickly as she could.

"Oh, honey." Bianca wrapped an arm around Terra's shoulders and squeezed. "That's a tough one, isn't it? Listen ... this is all kind of a mess right now. But we'll get it sorted out. I promise you. These things have a way of working themselves out."

"I don't... I can't..." Terra stopped, forcing herself to breathe past the pain that gripped her heart. She took a moment to collect her thoughts as she twisted a loose thread from the blanket around her finger. Ultimately, her pain didn't matter. Not really. That was part of the deal with being a leader to the Earth Fae. It had been drilled into her since a young age. She was but one person. The Earth Fae were thousands. As their leader, she had to make choices that best protected them, no matter what it meant for her personally. "It doesn't matter. Not really. I have to think about what's best for my people."

"But Terra..." Bianca began, and Terra shook her head, cutting her off.

"No, Bianca. I can't sacrifice my people in order to pursue my own personal needs. The reality is that Domnu will come back, and she's going to come after our amulet. I must secure it and get back to our world before she launches whatever her next step is in this battle of hers to rise to power. We can't forget — we're at war here."

"You're right." Bianca slapped her palms on her knees and then stood, biting her nail as she paced the room. "We got a little caught up in the romance of it all, but, knowing Domnu, she won't be away for long. She's impatient, impulsive, and obsessive. Which makes her, in some respects, largely unpredictable. The only thing we can rely upon is that she's coming back for the knife. We need to get the amulet back before she does."

"We do. I have an idea where it is," Terra said, tapping her chest. "I can feel it when I'm close. We're bonded."

"That's a nifty little feature, isn't it then?" Bianca pursed her lips. "Get the knife, get off the island, then deal with your brother? And Rian?"

"Unfortunately, I think that needs to be the way of it. Domnu isn't going to stop. She's making her way through all of the Elemental Fae in her quest to overthrow her sister. Families, huh?" Terra's eyes fell to where her brother lay bruised and battered on the floor. "They're a bit tricky, aren't they?"

"That's an understatement." Bianca paused in her pacing. "Listen... I think I may have something that can help us down the road. Maybe not immediately, but I've been researching ways that we can maybe disarm or neutralize Domnu, and I might have found something. It's an ancient ritual."

"Where did you find it?" Terra asked, hope blooming in her chest. "Is it the same as what Lily found?"

"In the library at the castle. Well, Lily and I found it. They let us into the records room. I've actually seen it mentioned twice, first in a book that King Callum gave me and the second time in a book that I found in the library. It would require, well, great sacrifice."

"Which is?"

"I believe, if I'm interpreting it correctly, that the

Elemental Fae would be required to melt their amulets together. In doing so, the combined power can create a set of golden cuffs that will bind Domnu's powers indefinitely."

"Our amulets?" Terra's hand went to her chest in shock. As long as she'd ever known it, the one who carried the amulet ruled the people. Without it ... how would power be transferred? Was it even possible to use them in such a manner?

"I know. It's a big ask. And I wouldn't bring it up unless we had no other choice. But she's gaining momentum, isn't she? She's infiltrated several of the royal houses, she's creating chaos all over the place, and the more she stirs the pot — well, the worse it is going to get. I think you'll need a unified front to take her down once and for all."

"The Air Fae are next, aren't they?"

"If they're not already under siege," Bianca agreed. "I think, when we get out of here, we need to call a meeting with King Callum and Lily. We need to take this option seriously because I don't think Domnu's ever going to stop. She'll go quiet for a few decades at a time, but she'll never stop. We have to be the ones to stop her."

"Well at least it's a step forward." Terra stood. "That gives me hope that there is more to be done once we get off this island."

Cormac stirred, his eyes fluttering open, and jolted upwards when his awareness returned. Terra resisted the urge to go to him, to help him rise, when he shifted on the floor and cursed. Bringing his hand to his ribs, he tried to stand, but fumbled back against the wall. Cormac raised pleading eyes to Terra.

"Sister. I know you can ease my pain."

It wasn't even a request. Cormac just assumed that Terra would help him. Because that's what she always did — helped everyone. As leader of the Earth Fae, it was her duty to help a fallen Fae. And yet. He was also guilty of betrayal and subject to exile. Duty warred with desire, but, still, she did nothing.

"That's an interesting way of phrasing it. You're right, Cormac. I can take the pain. I've been taking the pain that you bestowed upon me by allowing my estrangement from the family for years now. Every day, I've sat with that pain while you've lived a lie. So now, brother, I believe it is time for you to take the pain."

"Terra," Cormac whined, wincing once more as he struggled to rise. "It *really* hurts. I think my ribs are broken."

"Good," Terra surprised herself by saying. Never had she been so callous with her brothers before, even when they'd fought. Now, she found she didn't care anymore. She loved Cormac, but she didn't care about his needs at this moment. He'd proven himself untrustworthy, and now she needed to focus on what was best for her people, not for just her brother. Maybe she was a bit bitter, or maybe she was just hurt, but she realized with sudden stark clarity that family was just a word — it didn't mean sacrificing her needs for others. What Terra wanted mattered too. And right now? She wanted her damn knife back. "Maybe you'll learn something from this."

"Terra? What's gotten into you? You've changed."

Cormac hissed as he finally managed to stand, though he was bent almost at the waist in pain.

"Maybe I have," Terra agreed. "And that's a good thing, isn't it? People don't stay the same, Cormac. They change, and grow, and learn. Something you could take note of. That's what happens when new information is discovered. Now that I know who you really are, I'll no longer waste my time grieving the loss of you in my life. All those hours wasted, crying because I missed you ... well, no more. Because the person I thought I missed wasn't the real you anyway. Now that you've shed your skin, you've also given me freedom. I'm free from ever worrying about you again."

"That's harsh, Terra. What happened to forgiveness? And people making mistakes?" Cormac asked.

"There's mistakes. And then there's deliberate cruelty. I don't think you've made a mistake, Cormac. I think you're just angry that the consequences finally caught up with you."

With that, Terra left the cottage, no longer able to look at Cormac's broken and bruised face. She'd already grieved the loss of him once, but now the grief that hit her was so wildly different. Before it had been for the brother she'd loved, but now it was for the understanding that he'd never loved *her* at all.

"Make sure he doesn't leave," Terra instructed Callahan who stood outside the door. Technically, he probably was stationed there to make sure she didn't leave either, but he made no move to stop her as she walked away.

"Not a problem, Lady Terra."

17

"I'VE GOT JUST the thing for you, boyo," Callahan said when Seamus and Rian returned from their walk. Seamus, much to Rian's surprise, hadn't tried to speak to him. He seemed to understand that Rian's emotions were too raw in that moment, and instead, he had quietly kept pace with Rian as he'd walked off his head of anger.

Well, not really. The anger always lived with him, didn't it? But at the very least, Rian had been able to calm himself down enough so that he didn't return to the cottage and rip Cormac's head off his shoulders, though he fantasized about it in grisly detail while they'd plodded through misty late-afternoon light. Even more interesting? Rian was just as incensed about Cormac hurting Terra as he was about the role the man had played in his exile.

Which, in itself, messed with his head.

"What's that?" Rian eyed Callahan.

"Whiskey. And a fire." Callahan gestured to where he'd built a bonfire in front of the cottages and had pulled some benches over beneath a few trees clustered together that would provide some shelter from the rain that still misted lightly down. Night had drawn close, and, despite himself, Rian's eyes tracked to the cottages, searching for Terra.

"Where are the women?" Seamus asked.

"Together in your cottage. Cormac has been restrained in Terra's. He sleeps now." Callahan's gaze danced across Rian's cut lip. "He'll live."

"That's too bad." Rian sneered.

"Perhaps," Callahan shrugged, pragmatic as always.

"In that case, whiskey would be welcome," Seamus said, moving to stand by the fire. Rian joined him, holding his hands out to the blaze, the wind carrying the melancholy call of the sea with it.

"I've plenty of it, for just such a moment, as well as some sausage rolls to heat over the fire." At that, Rian turned and shot Callahan a questioning look.

"Sausage rolls?"

"You're not the only one with magick. But your disgusting amount of wealth also helps in the matters. I'm well stocked, as I wasn't sure how long we'd be on this desolate rock in the ocean."

"It's beautiful here," Seamus said. He accepted a camping enamel mug from Callahan and grinned his thanks when the man poured the whiskey, the firelight catching the amber tones of the liquid. "Thanks for that."

"Of course." Callahan repeated the same for Rian, and soon the three of them sat on the benches, their feet outstretched to the fire, sausage rolls warming at the edge of the flames.

"You'll need to save one for Bianca or she'll be having my head," Seamus said, gesturing to a roll with his mug.

"There's plenty. I'll be seeing to the ladies, no worries on that," Callahan promised. Rian downed his cup in two fiery swallows and filled his mug to the brim once more. The fire crackled and popped, and Rian tapped his finger idly against his mug as his thoughts whirled.

"How do you do it?" Rian looked up, surprised to realize the question had sprung from him.

"Do what?" Seamus asked, realizing that Rian was looking at him.

"Be a good partner to Bianca. Go to battle with her and not lose your mind that she'll get hurt. Let her lead when she needs to lead. Just ... that. All of that." Rian spit out before slugging another mouthful of whiskey.

"Ingrate," Callahan muttered, annoyed at how Rian was drinking his nice whiskey.

"Are you asking me how to be in a relationship, Rian?" Seamus pretended to check his nails and fluttered his eyelashes at Rian as though they were girls gossiping at a sleepover.

"Eat shite," Rian said. He should have known better than to bring up his concerns.

"Come on, man, I'm just playing. In all seriousness? It's hard. It takes constant work. Every time we go into battle, I have to just remember that she is an adult who can make her own choices. There is no way that I can hold her back, as my woman is a powerful force in her own right. I just have to trust she'll make good decisions."

"Plus she'd knock your head off your shoulders if you

stopped her from fighting for the Good Fae," Callahan added. "Quite a woman you have there, Seamus."

"It's a lucky man, I am," Seamus agreed. "I've known it from day one. I just needed to convince her to pick me. Once I had my chance, I never let go."

"I had my chance. I walked away," Rian admitted. Silence fell, and he studied the flames dancing in the fire as though he could find the answer buried deep in the embers.

"I mean ... she's right there. You could just turn around and go back." Seamus broke the silence and gestured with his mug to the cottages. Rian stared at him, dumbstruck, and Callahan snorted.

It was the snort that did him in.

Soon, the three men were laughing so hard that tears ran down Rian's cheeks. Maybe it was because he hadn't eaten food that day and the whiskey was going to his head a bit, but that had to be one of the funniest things he'd ever heard. When they finally quieted, Rian shook his head and wiped his eyes.

"You make it sound so easy. Sure and I wish it could be. It's not ... the truth of it is ... I'm not good enough for her."

"I don't know about that," Seamus said, "isn't that how all men feel when they find themselves with an amazing woman? Like they're trying to hold onto a rainbow? I think, if she picks you, then you have to trust her to know her own mind in what she wants."

"Well said." Callahan tapped the rim of his mug to Seamus's.

Rian huffed out a laugh and shifted, picking up a stick to nudge the sausage rolls a bit.

"You make it sound so simple."

"And you overcomplicate things," Callahan said. Rian glanced at his friend, the one person he allowed close in his life.

"Do I? You *know* me. You know the things that I've done. The wrongs that weigh on my conscience. I've systematically tried to hurt the Earth Fae in any manner that I can since I've been exiled. I've even made a deal with the Dark Fae. Don't tell me that I'm good enough for a pure heart like Terra. I'm not, and you well know it."

"And yet she chooses you," Seamus said.

"She might not know ... she doesn't understand what I really am, you see?"

"Maybe she thinks you're worth saving," Callahan's voice carried across the fire and cracked like a whip across Rian's back. His shoulders tensed.

"I think we both know I'm too far past that," Rian finally bit out. Once more, he filled his cup, while the men again fell silent. The wind wailed its sullen song, rambling across the fields, while the waves crashed below. It was a cold night, colder than it had been since they arrived, and Rian couldn't help but feel like the weather mirrored how he felt inside.

"Is that right? You've just decided it then? You let the Earth Fae exile you and decide since they say you're bad, well, then you'll be bad? You've got an amazing woman in there who is willing to take a chance on you and you're going to throw that away because you've convinced yourself that you're not a good person? I didn't realize your mother had raised a damn fool," Callahan said.

"Don't you dare speak of my mother," Rian rose, and Callahan stood, meeting him.

"Oh, but I will. You scare everyone else, but remember, Rian — I bow to no man, and I'll speak exactly what I think, even if you don't like what I have to say. Your mother would be ashamed of you."

Rian raised a fist but stopped just short of punching Callahan in the face, his arm shaking with the effort to restrain himself. His breath caught in his chest, and his stomach twisted when Callahan smiled and lifted his chin in challenge.

"Real bad guy, aren't you?" Callahan asked, taunting him, the light of war in his eyes. Rian wanted nothing more than to smash that smile off the man's face. But he couldn't, he just couldn't.

"Rian."

At Terra's voice behind him, Rian closed his eyes.

"Go to your woman, Rian. You gain nothing by walking away and everything by staying. What will it be?"

"Rian ... what's going on?" Terra asked again, her voice tender and insistent behind him. Once more, she'd arrived before he could step past a line he couldn't come back from.

"Do not speak of my mother," Rian ground out.

"I absolutely will speak of her. Because if you can't remember her last words to you, I'll be here to remind you of them."

Furious, Rian turned to the fire, ignoring Terra for a moment as he struggled to compose himself. His emotions roiled inside him, and he felt like a man lost at sea, barely hanging onto a threadbare life ring while the waves threatened to drag him under. Every time he came up for a breath, another emotion seemed to crash over him, and he couldn't see his way forward.

"Rian. Can I speak with you?" Terra's voice, like a beam of light from a lonely lighthouse, shone into his darkness. Rian dug his nails into his palms, trying to force himself to be calm. His pain wasn't for her to manage. Finally, he gave a curt nod, and bent down to pick up his cup, filling it once more with whiskey. Turning, he followed Terra who walked toward his cottage, nerves dancing through him at the thought of being alone with her.

"Why do I smell sausage rolls?" Bianca demanded from behind him, and Seamus's laughter followed Rian on the misty night air. He'd been right about his woman, Rian thought, and realized he was just a bit jealous of Seamus's easy relationship with Bianca. Though Seamus had said it was hard, it certainly didn't look that way from the outside.

Terra stood at his door, a touch of uncertainty playing across her face, and he motioned for her to go inside. Rian hated that he was responsible for bringing her anything less than joy. Was it their fated mate bond that had turned him so quickly from wanting to hand her over to the Dark Fae to now wanting to cradle her close like she was the most precious gift in the world? He'd been fascinated by her since the moment he'd seen her, that was true enough, but still he'd been willing to broker a deal with Domnu without worrying too much for Terra's fate. When had that changed? Had it been their first kiss? Or had it been the moment he'd caught her speaking softly to a ladybug and helping it find its way to a clover flower? There was a softness and sweetness to Terra that appealed to his protective instincts.

But in this moment — the only one she needed protecting from was him.

"Rian..." Terra began, crossing the room with her hands clasped in front of her as though she was a school-teacher about to deliver a lecture. Her words skidded to a stop as she stared at something on his bed. Curious, he crossed to her side to see what had caused her to falter.

Terra reached out and gently lifted the silly flower garland that he'd won from the game the other night. He'd kept it, foolishly he supposed, and draped it on a corner of the bed. It was but a bit of sentimentality from a brief moment in time where he'd felt normal once more — like he belonged with a group of friends. It wasn't real, as they hadn't chosen to be by his side, instead they'd merely been passing time while he'd kept them prison-ers. The reality of the situation far outweighed the pretty picture he'd tried to make of it in his head, and now he felt stupid for keeping the flower chain.

"Oh, *Rian*." Terra pursed her lips, reaching up to brush her fingers across his cheek before he could step back. "Why won't you let me love you?"

Rian caught her hand, pulling it away from his face, but he didn't let go. Instead, he stared down at her sad eyes, his chest heaving with the effort to restrain himself. A tangled web of energy connected the two. Rian could almost reach out and touch it. Curiosity bloomed, as a warm languid heat pulsed through his body. What would it be like to lie with Terra? To love Terra? By any indication, it would be earth shattering. He'd heard the same through the years, from those lucky enough to find their fated mates. The connection was both intense and soul warming

The problem was, Rian wasn't sure he had a soul left. He was a dried husk of a man, with no sustenance left to give Terra, and he'd do her a disservice by accepting what she offered. And yet, he stood, transfixed, as her eyes pleaded with him.

He couldn't move forward.

But he couldn't leave either.

Frozen, Rian waited, his focus narrowing until all he could see were the flecks of gold in Terra's hypnotic emerald eyes. Seeming to understand what he needed, Terra's lips eased into a soft smile.

She stepped forward.

18

THE MAN WAS CRYING out for love.

Why couldn't he see that what he needed wasn't world domination or vengeance? His heart cried out for family. For love. For *her*. She could give this to him, if only he'd let her. Terra knew what it was like to lose those she loved. Together, they could heal each other's wounds, and create their own family. If only...

Boldly, she walked to Rian and nudged him until the back of his knees hit the side of the bed and he dropped to the mattress. Terra had brought him here to ask him, plainly, to give her the knife back. But now she realized that maybe she'd brought him here for something else as well. If he'd only give her this small moment in time together, then she was going to take it, because never again would she know the touch of her fated mate — or another man. If Rian left her, after this, she'd live the rest of her days alone and untouched, forever pining for him. It was both the blessing and the curse of a fated mate bond. How much of himself would he give to her?

She needed to show him what they could be to each other.

Rian's hands were clenched in fists on his knees, and Terra nudged his legs open with her body, so she stood between his thighs. Still, he didn't touch her. Instead, a fine tremble worked its way through his body as though it took everything in his power to remain still. What would it take to make him lose control? Reaching out, Terra threaded her fingers through his thick hair, and he surprised her by bringing his forehead to her stomach. She held him there, one hand lightly tangled in his hair, the other stroking the thick bands of muscles that ridged his shoulders. Her eyes caught on the simple floral garland, a whimsy that he'd kept, and she held on tight to the knowledge that beneath this tough exterior lay a heart that was still capable of love.

He shifted, just the slightest of movements, and Terra closed her eyes softly and exhaled in relief when his arms came around her waist. Now, too, he explored her body much like she did his, stroking softly, as they held each other through the storm of emotions that threatened to engulf them both. Her body hummed with energy, the thread of magick inside of her recognizing his, and she braced her hands on his shoulders and lifted herself to straddle him. When he made no move to stop her, instead continuing to lightly stroke his hands up and down her sides, Terra took it as a win.

"Rian," Terra said softly, and when he tilted his head to look up at her, his eyes filled with need, she captured his lips with her own. Gently, ever so gently, she breathed against his mouth, the warmth and spiciness of his taste dancing across her lips. When he groaned lightly into her kiss, Terra smiled. There was no way he didn't feel what she felt.

It was as though they were two lovers caught in time, the world falling away around them, and the only thing that mattered was the two of them, locked away in this cottage. The single flickering candle lit the room, bathing them in soft light, but very little warmth. Not that Terra needed warmth. Her body felt energized, alive, and heightened to touch. Trails of heat followed Rian's fingertips as he stroked her body, and her hips moved against him of their own accord, rolling against his hardness. Terra whimpered into his mouth, the intensity of his desire igniting a flame inside her. No longer did she want to linger over each brush of her lips on his. She wanted to devour him whole. Need made her tug at the canvas coat he wore, wanting to feel her skin against his.

"Terra ... we can't..." Rian began, and a flash of anger almost made Terra scream in frustration. Instead, she gripped his chin with her hands and narrowed her eyes at his stubborn and beautiful face.

"No, Rian, not *we*. You. It's you who holds yourself back from receiving love that is offered. Not me." Her breath came out in angry little pants, and she was so turned on that stars danced in front of her eyes, and still she waited, needing him to accept what she offered.

"I don't know how to accept it." His words were muffled where he'd buried his face in her neck, and her anger eased at his admission.

"Let me show you then." Once more, she lifted his chin, and this time she kissed him with all of the love she had. Opening herself, she lost herself in the kiss, her heart singing when he angled his head and kissed her back. This time it was Rian who took, gripping her tightly as he kissed her like a man starved. Terra arched against him, his arms pinning her to his body, and began to rock her hips, needing to feel him against her.

Once he'd given in, something seemed to shift in Rian, and he rolled, surprising Terra with his strength as he lifted her in his arms, cradling her as though she was the tiniest of beings. Now, with their positions shifted, Rian reared over her and quickly divested himself of his clothes so that he stood before her in all his naked beauty. And goddess, was the man beautiful, Terra thought, drinking in the sight of the sinewy muscles that ranged across his chest and down to his tapered waist. His desire was evident, and lust pooled low in her stomach as she drank in the sight of her glorious fated mate, ready for her.

"Have I told you how beautiful you are?" Rian danced his fingertips over her ankle, causing a shiver to zip along her sensitive skin. "How thoughts of touching your soft body keeps me up at night?"

"Um..." Terra's mind short-circuited for a second when he pulled her dress up and straight over her head, leaving her hands entangled in her sleeves over her head. Her skin burned as his gaze traced her skin, and she arched her back, offering herself to him like a gift to a god.

"Nothing compares," Rian whispered, and moved to kneel between her legs. He trailed his hands up the outside of her muscular legs and then spread them wider.

For a moment, he stilled, drinking in the sight of her spread before him in supplication, and Terra had never been more turned on in her life. "Nothing. There will never be another woman who walks this earth that is as stunning as you, Terra. Perfect and pure Terra."

The way he said the last part had an edge to it that Terra dearly wanted to examine, but Rian took that moment to bury his face between her legs, and, when his mouth found her, liquid and hot, she thought no more. Instead, Terra became a woman of need and sensation, responding to his every touch, his whispered commands, his careful examination of every lick, tug, and stroke that elicited a response from her. Rian dedicated himself to the art of loving her the same way he did anything else in his life, with a careful, controlled, and single-minded focus that very quickly took Terra from merely wanting him to begging for release as he lapped at her like she was an ice cream cone on a hot summer's day. Only when she'd finally exploded into pleasure, ecstasy causing her limbs to shake and her chest to heave with desire, did he ease back and lean over her, a satisfied smile on his face.

"You, Terra, are like the first hint of spring after a long icy winter."

Terra's heart almost melted in her chest, and she wanted to weep for this broken man who seemed to be saying goodbye to her in the same moment he was welcoming her home. She understood what he was doing, even if she didn't agree with it, and all she could do was hold onto him tighter and hope she'd be able to convince him that she'd never turn her back on him.

Reaching up, she took his hand and pulled it to her chest.

"Do you feel that Rian?"

"Terra..." Rian shifted above her, uncomfortable.

"It's you and I, Rian. Nobody else. We're meant for each other, destined across time, chosen by the Fates themselves. We matter. *This* matters." His hand against her skin was warm, and she wondered if he even realized that he brushed his thumb lightly in time to the beat of her heart.

"How can you be so sure? Rian asked. "Maybe they got it wrong..."

"Does this feel wrong to you?" Terra brought his hand to her lips, kissing his palm gently as though she was blessing it, and his eyes closed. She knew he felt what she did. Their love was sacred and powerful, and he only had to claim her. Together they could fight the darkness and forge a new way forward.

But she couldn't force him. All Terra could do was love Rian and show him the way. Tugging his arms, she pulled him, so he lay on top of her, the weight of him surrounding her and making her feel safe. Secure. Desired. Opening herself for him, Terra gasped and arched against his body as he entered her in one swift motion, hard to her soft, pinning her beneath him. He filled her in a way that no other had, and now her body sang, coming to life, and her heart ached for her to complete the ritual.

To claim him in full.

Dare she claim him even if he didn't claim her back? Yes, her heart all but sobbed, yes, yes, yes. He moved against her, slick and warm, sliding in and out of her heat, and then she could think no more as he took her over the crest, and waves of sweet pleasure crashed through her body. She held on, whispering words of love in his ear, as he drove into her, mindless, needing her as much as she needed him, until at last, they came together, and he collapsed to her side.

Immediately, Terra curled into him, not wanting to break contact, knowing he was already pulling away from her. When his arm looped around her waist, she smiled, though tears hovered, unshed, at her eyes.

"I'm not good enough for you. I'll never be good enough for you. I've done bad things, Terra. I don't deserve your love," Rian whispered.

There was nothing to say. She'd already told him what she wanted, no, *needed* from him, and he'd convinced himself that he was committed to a path he'd already set for himself. When his soft breathing filled the room, Terra realized he'd fallen asleep in her arms. She trembled, scared for the choice she was about to make, and what it would mean for her life. Leaning closer, Terra placed a hand to Rian's chest. She closed her eyes and found her magick, feeling it shimmer and dance in excitement, and then she let it flow.

"I claim you, Rian, as my fated mate. Now, forever, and ever on. You will have my love."

Light flashed in the room, and Terra shivered, knowing it was done.

She dearly hoped she hadn't just signed her death sentence.

19

RIAN AWOKE, unsure of where he was for a moment, filled with a bone-deep contentment for the first time in, well, ever. His mind flashed back to the glory of making love to Terra, the visual reel playing out in a loop in his mind, and he found himself stiffening in response. He needed her again and immediately.

A soft noise had him freezing in place. Shifting his eyes, the sight that greeted him immediately washed away the contentment he'd so been enjoying. Terra knelt on the floor, a wood plank removed and set aside, and peered into the hole. She was going after her amulet, Rian realized, and quickly understood that everything from last night had been a lie. She'd used sex to disarm him, fully intending to get her amulet back. His calculating side applauded her — hadn't he very much done the same when he'd first stolen it from her? But his other side, his vulnerable self who had only just started to peek out from behind the walls he'd built, was devastated.

It was better this way, Rian silently lectured himself,

schooling his breathing so he could tamp down on any impulsive responses that he might have. If anything, Terra handed him a gift right now. She was making it much easier to carry out the task that he had promised he would do. It wasn't in Rian's nature to go back on his word, and, while he'd started to consider it where Terra was concerned, now he wouldn't have to. Sliding from the bed, he padded, naked and silent to her side and grabbed her wrist just before she touched the iron box and burned her hand. Terra squealed in surprise and tumbled back on that gorgeous bum of hers he'd so enjoyed touching the night before.

"Is that the way of it then?" Rian asked, angling his head to nod at the box and then back to Terra's startled face. "Blind me with sex and steal the amulet back."

"No, that's not the way of it," Terra said, crossing her arms over her chest and poking out her bottom lip. A lip he dearly wanted to bite. "I wanted to know if it was still there, but I planned to ask you for it when you woke up."

"Why not ask me to retrieve it for you then? You have to know that this doesn't look good for you." Like a kid caught with her hand in the candy jar.

"I didn't want to wake you, Rian. I know you've been having restless nights, and you were so peaceful. Maybe I shouldn't have gone looking for it, but I was going to ask you for it back, Rian. I promise you. You've already expressed that we're to take you at your word, so now I'll ask you to take me at mine." There was no subterfuge in Terra's expression as she looked at him with a steady and clear gaze. He reminded himself that this was a woman who had sat by his mother's side when she'd died and had lost her family in her quest to find answers for him. Would she now lie? It seemed out of character for her, and he crouched, torn on how to proceed.

"You would have burned your hands. The box is iron," Rian pointed out.

"I can see that now. I was just getting the faintest pulse that the knife was near, and I wanted to see if that was really the case. I wouldn't have touched iron. I know we're in danger here and injuring myself is not in my best interest."

Confusion roiled in Rian and without another word he reached in and pulled the box out, tossing it on the floor by Terra like someone grabbing a hot coal from the fire. He stood, crossing the room to dress quickly as he felt vulnerable being naked near the iron, and tried to figure out his next move.

"Thanks for sex last night. It was fun," Rian said, deliberately careless with his tone. A shudder ran through him at his words, and he couldn't bring himself to look at Terra's face. Frankly, he was disgusted with himself, but that wasn't necessarily a feeling he was unfamiliar with.

"Fun," Terra echoed softly. When he turned, fully dressed, with his weapons strapped at his sides, he found her with her shoulders slumped, staring into the hole in the floor. It was so at odds with the powerful and confident woman that she was, that disgust filled him like a sticky sludge. He'd done this to her. He'd taken a beautiful and powerful woman and had hurt her.

Shame. He could all but hear his mother's whisper in his head.

Working quickly, Rian picked up the cloth and wrapped it around the box, unlocking the lock with the combination, as well as disarming the magick spell around it. Though his hands burned, the cloth did its job, and no blisters formed. Flipping the lid back, he pointed to the knife that nestled in the bottom of the box.

"See? It's here. Safe as can be."

Terra turned, not meeting his gaze, and looked down at the knife.

"May I have it?" Terra asked, a tremble in her voice.

Shouts arose outside, startling them both.

"Rian! Domnua!" Callahan shouted. Rian was on his feet and at the door in seconds. Cracking open the door, he saw the Goddess Domnu strolling across the field, hundreds of Domnua at her back. Though he had intended to give her the knife, when he looked from the Goddess and back to where Terra sat on the floor, watching him as though she could read the secrets of his soul, he froze. He didn't trust the Goddess, Rian realized. But he *did* trust Terra. At the moment, the safest bet would be giving her the amulet back. She couldn't leave the island without him releasing the magickal wards, and she would do anything to protect the Earth Fae's amulet from harm. Until he could determine what to do about Domnu, it was best the knife went back to Terra.

At least that was the reasoning he gave himself.

"Yes, you may have it back. For now." Rian took two steps across the room and reached in and retrieved the knife, making sure his fingers didn't brush the edges of the iron box.

"Really?" Terra asked, hope dawning on her gorgeous

face. She held out her hands, and he dropped the amulet into her palms before he could change his mind. Her mouth parted, and a sheen of tears glinted as her fingers closed around the hilt. She looked at it like a mother welcoming her baby into her arms, Rian realized, before more shouts drew his attention.

"Stay inside. Domnu fully expects to have the amulet handed to her, and she'll happily kill to get it."

"What are you going to do?" Terra asked, standing and slipping the knife into the pocket of her dress.

"I don't know," Rian admitted. "Stall. Delay. Distract. I can't... I can't think straight. I was so certain I knew what I wanted when I agreed to all of this, and now—"

"It's okay to change your mind, Rian. While I appreciate your commitment to keeping your word, does that really apply when you're dealing with an insidious devil beast who only keeps her end of the bargain if it suits her? Have no doubt that Domnu would just as easily lie to you as she would be truthful. She doesn't make deals with a code of honor, she makes deals with a code of self-preservation."

"Understood. Stay put." Rian ordered and slipped out the door. For good measure, he used his magick to lock the door behind him and added an extra shield to prevent Terra from leaving the cottage. He could only deal with one thing at a time, and until he figured out what to do next, he needed to know she was safe.

That the *knife* was safe, he meant. That was all that mattered. Terra was ... an enjoyable distraction, or so Rian lied to himself. That was all she had to be.

"Ah, there he is. My little outcast." Goddess Domnu

purred, and her serpent hair bared their fangs in laughter. Her black lace dress hugged her considerable assets, and her nails were sharpened to resemble talons. "I presume you have the Earth Fae's amulet for me?"

Callahan peered at him from where he stood by the fire that still burned from the night before. Rian didn't doubt that the man wanted nothing more than to reach into the flames and throw burning coals at the Goddess. Knowing he needed to distract her before one of the others set her off, Rian walked forward until he stood close to the Goddess. Her guards didn't like that, and he realized he'd probably broken some sort of protocol by walking directly up to her. However the move seemed to intrigue her, and a smile dawned on her face.

"Bold one, aren't you?" Domnu tapped one of her nails on his chest. "You'd make a great lover, I'm certain of it."

"I don't have the amulet to give you," Rian said, not wanting Domnu to explore the direction she was going regarding him being her lover.

"Is that so? Disappointing." Domnu pursed her lips and studied Rian for a moment, and once again he was struck by the madness that twirled in her soulless black eyes. "Walk with me."

"Of course," Rian said, falling into step next to her. Anything to take the Goddess farther away from the encampment.

"I like you, Rian," Goddess Domnu said, hooking her arm though his as though they were merely having a casual morning stroll to enjoy the weather. Which, Rian noted, was lovely this morning. He suspected it was

Domnu's doing. She didn't seem like the type of woman who would tolerate rain messing up her outfit. He tilted his head slightly away from the snakes that coiled around her head. "I've very much enjoyed your campaign to retaliate against the Earth Fae. It's been fun for me to watch, and I suspect we are kindred spirits."

A bitter taste filled Rian's mouth, and he ground his teeth together. What had his life come to that the Goddess of all things dark and decrepit thought they were very much alike? His shoulders slumped. She wasn't wrong, either. He had done some pretty awful things to the Earth in order to seek revenge. Feeling guilt over his actions hadn't stopped him from doing the same again. Instead he'd just buried his remorse. What did that make him? A bad person. Just like the Earth Fae had deter-mined him to be. It was a good reminder for Rian, as he'd momentarily lost his head with Terra, as well as the others. This was just a brief moment in time, where Rian could pretend like he was the person he used to be. Fun, unencumbered, hopeful for the future.

Goddess Domnu drew to a stop at the edge of the cliff, and together they looked down at Cathedral Rocks, the pillars splitting the ocean and towering toward the sky.

"We could be like those rocks, you and I. Strong, stat-uesque, remarkable," Goddess Domnu mused, and Rian realized just how deep he was in if the Goddess was considering him as a potential mate. Oily disgust slid through Rian's gut as he thought about the sweetness of Terra opening herself for him and what Domnu now suggested to him. The two were night and day, cold to warmth, bitter to sweet. Even the thought of... Rian slid his glance to the snakes that slithered around Domnu's head ... nope, there was no way he'd ever be able to touch this monster.

"Look," Domnu continued. Throwing her hand up, she projected an image into the air, like watching a movie at an old-time drive-up movie theater. Rian blinked as the image of himself appeared, walking hand-in-hand with Goddess Domnu, across a barren land of dust and dirt. "This is our future, Rian, should you so choose it. We shall reign supreme, destroying the Earth as we go, enjoying our decadence as we see fit."

The image of a wasteland flipped to a concrete skyrise filled with sleek skyscrapers and not a green space to be seen. There, Rian watched himself luxuriate in a glittering penthouse apartment, complete with all the luxuries known to man, a bevy of servants at his beck and call.

"You'll be rich, powerful, with every whim catered to. Look how happy you are..." Domnu purred in his ear. He did look happy, Rian thought, as future Rian in the video threw back his head and laughed. There was a lightness in his face that he didn't now carry, and Rian briefly wondered if that was what would happen once vengeance was his.

"You see, Rian. Once you have it all ... you'll never live a day in darkness again. The real power comes from winning. The Earth Fae, they turned their backs on you. They ruined your life, your future, and left your mother to suffer. You have every right to your feelings, and your path for vengeance is a true one. Let me help you finish your goal. Revenge tastes so much sweeter when shared."

Domnu squeezed her hand at his bicep, and Rian closed his eyes, two sides warring inside him.

"I don't know anymore. What if revenge isn't the answer?" Rian rasped, knowing he could very well anger the Goddess with daring to question her. His life hung in a precarious balance, in more ways than one, and once more, he realized he stood at the edge of Cathedral Cliffs while life-changing decisions were made.

"Revenge is always the answer, Rian. You have to right the scales, don't you? Balance the injustices served against you. You'll never know peace if you don't have resolution to the travesty that's been served to you."

She wasn't likely wrong. Rian hadn't had a night of restful sleep since he'd been exiled. Except for ...last night that was. It was the first time he'd drifted off peacefully since the night of his trial.

The image in front of him shifted, drawing his attention, and his heart twisted.

His mother lay, thin and frail, in the wan morning light, on her deathbed. Alone, she cried for him, repeating his name over and over, railing against the injustices brought upon him by the Earth Fae.

"Your poor mother." Domnu's voice was soft — caring even. "Alone on her deathbed. The Earth Fae did this to her. To you. She knew no love in the end, no happiness. Why should you let them get away with it?" Domnu's voice lifted at the last moment, and when Rian turned to look down at her, she carried a smug look on the sharp angles of her face.

But this ... *this* was where she'd miscalculated.

His mother hadn't been alone when she'd died.

And she had known care, love, and nurturing.

Because Terra had been there.

It was then that Rian realized just how much of a pawn he was in Domnu's game. She was willing to rewrite history in order to get exactly what she wanted. She didn't care about Rian and his path to justice any more than she cared about the army of Domnua who blindly served her. Their lives mattered little to her, as did Rian's.

As would Terra's.

The thought of delivering Terra's beautiful soul into Domnu's wicked arms was enough to make his breath catch in his throat. While he understood he'd never be good enough for Terra — could never *really* have her as his partner — at the very least, maybe he could offer one small speck of redemption to her.

A gift, really. The only one he felt he was capable of giving.

"You're absolutely right, my Goddess. Thank you for showing me this, and our future together, in such a clear manner. Allow me to go collect the amulet, and the Earth Fae who protect it. I'll deliver them to you on a silver platter."

"I knew you'd see it my way," Domnu said, a delighted grin spreading on her face. "We're meant to be ... you and me. Like always recognizes like. It's been ages since I've had the taste of an Earth Fae on my lips, but now I find I can barely contain myself." Domnu trailed a finger across Rian's chest and simpered up at him. It was clear she wished for a kiss, but Rian couldn't stomach such a gesture. Instead, he dared to brush his thumb lightly across her lips, the snakes shivering around her head as he did so.

"I won't be long," Rian promised.

"See that you won't. I'm rarely patient, and you've already tested my limits."

"The best things come to those who wait." Rian blew her a kiss over his shoulder and jogged across the meadow, a sick feeling churning in his gut.

He hated what he had to do next, but his path forward was clear.

20

TERRA STOOD by the fire with Bianca and Seamus while Callahan patrolled the encampment. Though Rian had tried his hardest with his magickal skills to keep her locked in the cottage, it seemed he still forgot just who she was.

She was Terra, leader of the Earth Fae, and eminently powerful in her own right. She would no longer wait for her man to come to his senses, when she'd done all she could to show him that he could choose a different path for himself if he wanted. It was time for her to put her needs aside and focus on what was best for her people. Which, in this moment, meant she needed to protect her amulet so she could deliver it back to the Earth Fae to give them enough time to choose a new leader.

If Rian didn't claim her back, that is. Terra dearly hoped her gamble would pay off, otherwise she'd just put a time limit on her life. Unrequited claims from a fated mate resulted in a sickness that would eventually claim the life of the claimant. Another tricky Fae rule that was implemented in order to make sure Fae only made one claim in their lives.

She had planned to tell Rian this morning that she had claimed him the night before. Terra sensed that Rian needed to know that someone had chosen to stand by him, but he'd awoken at an inopportune moment.

The amulet hummed happily at her side, and she patted it lightly, feeling complete now that it had returned. Terra wasn't entirely clear if Rian had believed her when she'd said she'd not meant to take it from him without asking, but she hadn't lied to him. She would have taken it from him without asking if he hadn't given it to her, not at that moment, but if Rian hadn't come around to his senses, Terra would have gone back for the knife at some point that day. She'd only been determining its location. It was a subtle difference, and maybe she was walking in the gray area of truth, but at the exact moment when Rian had caught her, she had not planned to take the knife. It didn't sit well with her, this game they were playing, but until Rian could stand in his own truth and accept their future together, Terra still had to protect her people.

"There he is," Callahan nodded to where Rian stormed across the field, ignoring the army of Domnua that stood at the far edge of the meadow. They'd hovered there all morning, in a weird type of stasis, as though they would only be brought to life if Goddess Domnu switched them on. It was creepy, albeit fascinating, to observe an entire body of people just standing rigidly straight, barely swayed by the wind.

"He sure likes to storm about, doesn't he?" Bianca

asked, and, despite the grave severity of the situation they found themselves in, a smile quirked at Terra's lips.

"It's his patented move," Callahan agreed. He crossed his arms over his chest as his eyes tracked Rian's movements. Terra suspected he missed little, though he pretended a casual nonchalance to their current state of affairs. "Storming, stomping, and an occasional shouted curse. It's very effective, though I think he only uses it to convince himself he's a bad guy."

"It's not a show for others then?" Terra couldn't keep her eyes off of Rian. There was a certain grace to the way he carried himself, like a panther prowling the meadow, and though she should be intimidated by the cold expression on his face, her heart was just happy that he was close. She supposed that was the way of the fated mate bond—much like the knife that hummed in contentment at her side — so too would she be content when Rian was close.

"It is at that. But the man has to convince himself as well, doesn't he?" Callahan nodded as Rian skidded to a halt in front of them. "How'd you get on with herself, then?"

"Not great," Rian admitted, and Callahan chuckled.

"Sure and that's to be expected, isn't it? She's a nasty beastie that one."

"I've come to a decision," Rian said, refusing to look at Terra. Her heart twisted, and nerves made her reach for the hilt of the knife.

"Well, get on with it then. Let's hear what you've decided for all of us." Callahan rocked back on his heels and laughed once more when Rian glowered at him.

"Don't give me that look, boyo. It's the way of it, isn't it? You're trying to play high and mighty with our futures, promising something you can't deliver, and we're just meant to fall in line?"

"That's not..." Rian pinched his nose and sighed, before tossing a glance over his shoulder.

"What decision have you made with the Goddess Domnu?" Terra's voice was steady, and finally Rian looked at her. Oh, his eyes. Terra's heart fell. His eyes were those of a man who had lost all hope. It killed her to see him this way, and instinctively she stepped forward. Only when he raised a hand in the air, as though to throw up an invisible wall between them, did she stop. *Still he refused her comfort*. Stubborn to the bitter end, this one.

"I've promised her that I will deliver you all and the amulet over to her." At Seamus's curse, Rian flicked his gaze over the group, keeping his voice steady. "I shall break this promise."

"Wait ... what? You're not going to turn us over?" Bianca asked, pitching her voice low in case any magicks were about.

"No." Rian said, his voice clipped. "I'm not."

"You're breaking your word?" Terra asked, surprised that he would do so. It was the right decision, if looking at the side of good and evil, but nevertheless she hadn't been certain which way he would fall.

"I am. And I need you all to listen carefully." Rian threw his arm in the air violently, as though he was yelling at them, and they all took a surprised step back. "I'm going to act very angry at you. You will pretend you are scared or angry back."

"Screw you!" Bianca shouted, throwing her hands in the air, immediately jumping into action. "You can't take us!"

"That's the ticket," Rian said, flailing his arms about a bit. "I've released the wards on the island. You need to transport off. Immediately. There's no time for discussion." Rian turned, his face deadly serious as he met Terra's questioning look. "You must go, Terra. Take the amulet with you. I'm freeing you to return safely to your people."

"But what about you?" Seamus shouted, causing Terra to start. She'd been lost in Rian's haunted look and had forgotten they were supposed to be acting. Forcing herself to push aside her innate instinct to go to Rian and wrap her arms around him, she pasted a glaring look on her face.

"I will stay," Rian shouted back, his face angry, "or she'll come after you."

Oh, Rian. *No.*

Terra's glare became real, as she now understood what Rian was doing. He was sacrificing himself for their safety, becoming a distraction so they could disappear safely with the amulet. It was a heroic and bold move and told her exactly what she'd thought about Rian all along.

Beneath that jagged and angry exterior lay a heart of gold.

"You will not do so," Terra walked forward, not having to pretend her anger now. She jabbed a finger into his chest, and he stumbled back a step, surprised at her forcefulness. "You don't get to throw yourself to the Dark Fae like some sacrificial lamb."

"Who do you think is in charge here, darling?" Rian raised an eyebrow at her. He swept his arms out to encompass the field. "In case you've forgotten, you're my captives. I abducted you. You have no say."

"Nevertheless, we'll be staying with you," Bianca shouted, stomping her foot. Terra was too angry to say anything, instead her chest heaving with the desire to throttle this dear, sweet, stupid man. Did he honestly think they were just going to leave him behind? Even after what they'd shared the night before, Rian still didn't believe that others could show up for him. He really didn't trust anyone, did he?

"But... I kept you captive. Against your will. Stole the amulet." Rian jabbed his finger in the air, a pink flush coming to his cheeks.

"Hardly a prison sentence boyo. I've been wanting a lovely vacation with my sweet. A cottage on an isolated island? It's been perfect, really." Seamus winked at Bianca, and she simpered up at him before she remembered they were supposed to be acting angry and terrified.

"How dare you give me time away with my hot husband?" Bianca screeched, and Terra found herself desperately torn between laughter and tears.

"You can't stay," Rian argued. "You *have* to go. And now. Your lives are in danger."

This was exactly why Terra had claimed Rian. A strange calmness slipped through her. She'd known he wouldn't believe himself worthy enough of her love, so she had to make the first move and show up for him. Now, as he prepared to sacrifice himself for their safety, Terra fell even more in love with him. Her heart swelled, and, for a moment, she closed her eyes and let the love fill her.

"No," Terra said, her voice soft but firm.

"Don't be stupid, Terra. You'll die!" Rian turned on her, the fury on his face real. Terra ignored him, instead crouching to unlace her boots so her feet could be bare against the ground. If they were going to battle, she needed to draw from the natural energy of the Earth for extra strength in her magick.

"I might. But still … you don't fight alone." Terra walked forward until she stood close enough to Rian to see the pain in his eyes.

"You don't get to tell me what to do. I'll send you out of here myself if I have to," Rian warned though a hint of desperation entered his voice. It was that thread of uncertainty that Terra held onto.

"You don't get to sacrifice yourself on some false notion that you're not good enough for me. For us." Terra turned and pointed at the group behind her who all nodded empathetically.

"She's got the right of it," Callahan added.

"This is…" Rian raked a hand through his hair and glanced over his shoulder to where Domnu approached. "Asinine. I won't argue this with you. Leave. Now."

When Terra just shook her head at him, her heart breaking for the internal battle he waged, Rian swore and turned to leave.

"I can't," Terra said, her voice barely a whisper.

"What do you mean you can't?" Rian shouted, fury crackling around his body like he'd been hit with lightning. "The wards are gone. You are just as strong in magicks as I am. *Go*."

"I can't," Terra repeated, stepping forward until she placed her hand on his chest. Rian looked down at her hand like it was a snake that had just bitten him. "I can't, because I've claimed you."

"You ... wait ... you can't..." Rian stuttered, his face blanching white. He grabbed her hand and threw it away from his body.

"I've claimed *you*. My fated mate. My love. And if you don't choose to forgive our people, and yourself, then I will die." Terra said it simply, and waited, content with the choices she'd made.

"Are you crazy? You can't just ... no, you can't. *Terra*." Her name was a plea at his lips, and still she stood, pulling at the energy of the Earth, feeling its calm magick soothe her. Patience in all things. There is a season for everything, Terra reminded herself. Rian's seeds had been planted long ago. The question was—would he let himself grow?

A roar sounded behind them, and Terra looked up to see that the Goddess Domnu had unleashed her army. The ground shook as they tore across the meadow toward them.

"A bit overkill, isn't it?" Bianca asked.

"She's always been one for the dramatics, hasn't she?" Seamus agreed, a cheerful note in his voice.

"Please go. Leave me. I'm not meant for your world anymore. Save yourselves. I'll handle the rest of this," Rian begged.

"That's not what friends do, Rian," Callahan squeezed his shoulder and turned to meet the attack.

"Terra," Rian begged, grabbing her shoulders. "You can take them with you. You have the power to save them. It's irresponsible you're being. Your lives matter more than mine. This is madness."

"I'm sorry, my love. You're going to have to get used to people showing up for you too." With that, Terra moved around him and stepped into the fray.

21

How could she do this to him?

This was Rian's first thought as Terra strolled into battle, as though her life meant nothing. To him. To her people. To the Earth.

She'd claimed him.

He wasn't worthy of her, not in the slightest, not when he'd spent years trying to wreak havoc on the planet and gain vengeance against the Earth Fae. And for some reason she saw some redeeming quality in him? She was basically asking him to forgive the Earth Fae their wrongdoings.

And himself.

When Terra dodged an arrow from the Domnua, fury lit Rian. He had a choice to make. He could self-flagellate for his sins by refusing Terra's love and leaning into his bitterness, or he could try something new.

Forgiveness. Gratitude, even.

A second chance lay at his feet. Did he pick it up and

hold it close, or did he turn his back on his only chance at happiness?

Movement distracted him, and he looked to the cluster of trees by the fire where the oddly brilliant rays of the sun dappled the leaves and shone through to the Earth. The rays danced and shimmered, playing between the branches and shadows, and warmth slipped into him.

"Where the sun shines through the trees, blessing the ground with light, I will always be. Remember me, and I will come to you."

His mother's words rose in his mind, and he steeled himself as he watched her love twirl among the trees, gently reminding him of his promise to seek happiness no matter the hand that he was dealt. He'd forgotten that promise. Or at the very least, shoved it aside in order to seek revenge. But now, everything became very clear.

If he was a man of his word, then he needed to stand by his promise to his mother before anyone else. Happiness awaited him. If Terra was willing to take a chance on him, then he would spend his life living up to the man she thought she saw in him.

Decided, Rian turned, and, letting out a roar, he jumped in front of Terra and threw out a wall of ice to freeze the advancing line of Domnua. With a flick of his hand, he shattered the ice over them, laughing as their bodies exploded into tiny silvery fragments.

"Welcome back," Callahan shouted, clamping a hand on his shoulder before racing into battle.

"Stay with these two," Rian ordered Terra. When a smile bloomed on her face, his heart skipped a beat, and he grabbed her around the waist and brushed his lips across hers. Energy crackled between them, and a lightness shone inside him where he'd felt nothing but darkness for so long. As Terra's love melted the walls that he'd locked his emotions behind, they all flooded him at once like some crazy kaleidoscope of feelings. He fed on it, taking that rush of emotions, and honed them into one purposeful goal. Find Domnu and take her down. "Let me take care of the Goddess. You take care of you. Understood?"

"Still ordering me around?" Terra laughed at him and patted him on the cheek. "You'll learn eventually."

Rian didn't have time to argue as another wave of Dark Fae approached. Instead, he tapped a finger on her lips.

"Be safe."

With that, Rian raced across the field, easily felling Domnua as he went, love fueling his mission to get to the Goddess and incapacitate her. He knew that he wouldn't be able to destroy her, for that required far more power than he alone could wield, but at the very least he could stun her into retreat long enough to ferry Terra and the others back to safety. He caught sight of the Goddess Domnu slipping down the path toward the small beach and swerved, kicking out the knee of a Domnua who tried to stop him on the way.

The ocean was in a frenzy when he skidded to a halt at the beach, chest heaving, his eyes darting across the sand until they lighted upon where Goddess Domnu stood, a tight smile on her face.

"I should have known it was too good to be true." Domnu shrugged one delicate shoulder, her hair writhing around her head. When the snakes saw him, they bared their fangs and hissed. "You Elemental Fae are too weak to be a match to a strong woman like me."

"Did you really think that I'd be willing to join you? You lead one of the dumbest armies in all the realms and do nothing but bring hate and sadness wherever you go. What could possibly make you think that I would want to hook myself to your vision of the future?" Rian deliberately wanted to anger the Goddess. If he could keep her here, and not focused on the battle above, he was certain the others would have enough magick to handle the army of Dark Fae.

"Dumb? Now, now. It isn't nice to call my pets names." Domnu pursed her lips and made a small tsking sound. "Though, admittedly, they aren't the best at thinking on their feet."

"Or at all?" Rian countered. Keeping her talking, he walked across the small beach, his boots sinking into the soft sand. Behind the Goddess, the ocean turned a dark blue, similar to when a storm was about to roll in, and silver flashed below the surface. Rian perked up at the sight. The Water Fae had come, bringing with them their power, and together they might actually be able to hold the Goddess off from getting to Terra and her amulet. At the end of the day, losing Rian as a companion wasn't going to bother Domnu all that much. But losing the amulet would. The longer he kept her distracted, the closer he hoped they would get to Terra making the right decision and transporting herself away with the amulet. He could go after her once she was safe and clear.

Maybe he should have told her that, Rian realized, as

one of Domnu's snakes spat venom at his feet as he neared. Behind Domnu, a Water Fae slipped its head quietly out of the choppy water, blinking its opalescent eyes at Rian, and made a come-hither motion with his hand. The message was clear. If Rian could back the Goddess closer to the water, then his water brethren would help.

The time for conversation was over. Before Domnu could continue speaking more, Rian pulled at his thread of magick and blasted a wave of icicles at her, using all of his pent-up rage and anger to attack her with icy spears. The Earth rumbled beneath his feet, responding to his attack and, to his surprise, the sand shifted beneath Domnu's feet.

"If you think you can best me with your silly child's play..." Domnu hissed at him, dancing backward and batting his ice daggers easily from the air. One made its way through, slicing off the head of a snake, and Domnu stopped in her tracks at the water's edge, her eyes wide with shock. "You did *not* just hurt my hair."

"Looks that way," Rian said, pointing to where the snake's head trembled in the sand at her feet. Domnu gaped at him in shock, so surprised was she that he had managed to actually hurt a bit of her, that she didn't notice the sand giving way beneath her feet. Rian welcomed the power, calling upon his Earthen roots, and the sand opened up, sucking Domnu to her knees. She screamed, furious with him, and when the Water Fae threw a silvery net over her shoulders from behind, Rian backed up.

Her face looked like death.

Whirling, Rian ignored Domnu's screams as she thrashed against the magickal net that the Water Fae had caught her in and raced for the cliffs where the battle still raged. His breath caught as he crested a hill in time to see Terra facing off with a circle of Domnua.

All of his friends were cornered.

They'd made a valiant effort, but still the Dark Fae poured forth, trampling over a meadow soaked with the silvery blood of their fallen compatriots, and Rian's breath caught as Terra dodged a blow from a Domnua. The Dark Fae exploded in a silvery pop, and she let out a cheer of delight before her eyes went round with fear.

Rian's heart stopped.

A Domnua had crept up behind her and stabbed her in the back. He could feel the pain as if it was his own. Was that part of the fated mate claim one part of his brain idly wondered as he raced across the field, stabbing any Dark Fae that dashed into his path. He needed to get to Terra before the other Domnua fell upon her.

He wasn't going to make it in time.

Screaming, Rian lifted his hands to send out a wave of magick as a Dark Fae lifted a blade over the back of Terra's neck. At his shout, Terra looked up, her impossibly beautiful eyes locking with his.

Time seemed to slow as the blade lowered, and though Rian had already sent out a wave of protective magick, he could see it shimmering across the meadow, a second too late, when a flash of movement caught his eye. In the last moment before the blade could render its killing blow, Cormac dove between it and Terra, taking the blade for his sister.

His body landed on top of Terra just as Rian's magick hit the rest of the Domnua surrounding her and eliminated them in one silvery explosion.

"Terra. Baby. Let me see," Rian skidded to a halt and dropped to his knees, pushing Cormac from where his still body pinned Terra to the ground. He couldn't care less if Cormac was dead, but his future hinged on if Terra was. When she moaned, rolling over in his arms and blinked those gorgeous eyes up at him, Rian's stomach twisted. He might actually be sick, he realized, and swallowed back the bile that rose in his throat at the thought of how close he'd come to losing her.

"Rian. Oh, *no.*" Terra struggled to sit up when she saw Cormac's body. "We have to help him. Rian, please."

"Terra..." Rian could see the shimmer in the air around Cormac, which indicated the soul had already left his body. He knew Terra could see it as well, but still she grabbed desperately at her brother's shoulders. "He's gone."

"No. Not like this. Oh no, Cormac. *No.* It wasn't supposed to be like this," Terra said, tears dripping down her face for the brother who had betrayed them both.

Who had ultimately saved her life.

And his.

When Rian shifted, he realized his hands were sticky, and his eyes widened at the blood on his hands. Terra's blood. Panic kicked up, and fury caused him to turn and stand. They needed a moment of peace in this battle to heal Terra or Rian could truly lose his mind.

Standing, he shouted for the others, as he turned and faced the army.

"Mother Earth, oh wondrous and magickal being, I call upon your powers now to shift the balance from dark to light. The one who has endlessly nurtured you and stood for you is hurt. Will you not help her as she has helped you?" With that plea, Rian raised his hands and pulled the Earth's magick through him and sent a wave of it across the field. Much like the magick that Terra had used in their game the other day, the grass reached up, catching the Dark Fae as they ran, and pulled them into the Earth. Their screams were the last thing Rian heard before silence fell upon the meadow.

"Well, that was effective," Bianca commented as she skidded to a halt by his side, blood matting her blonde hair.

"She's hurt," Rian said, and dove for Terra to catch her before she slumped to the ground. Her body trembled in his arms, and tears coursed down her cheeks. Rian pulled her onto his lap, cradling her as she wept for her brother, worry for her injury coursing through him. "Terra, love. You're losing a lot of blood. You need to let us heal you."

"I ... he's gone. Cormac's gone. And the last words I said to him were in anger," Terra wept into her palms. Her breath came in short gasps, and, when she jerked in his arms, Rian realized she wasn't just sobbing — she was struggling to breathe.

"Callahan. Help," Rian looked to Callahan, who had a way with healing.

"I don't know that I can," Callahan said. He crouched by their side and ran his hands over Terra's arms, closing his eyes as he did. When he opened them, Rian wanted to punch his friend in the face. It was sorrow in his eyes.

"Don't say it," Rian warned.

"It might be too..." Callahan trailed off as Terra bowed in Rian's arms, losing consciousness.

"No, *no*. Absolutely not," Rian cried out. Standing with Terra in his arms, he whirled in a circle, his thoughts jumbling together like cars piling up on each other in an accident.

"Claim her," Bianca demanded, grabbing his arm so he looked down at her. "Claim her, Rian. It enhances your powers, doesn't it? *Claim her.*"

"I don't... I can't..." Rian couldn't think straight. He stumbled forward, the weight of Terra and the responsibility to save her growing heavy in his arms. Light caught his eye.

There, at the small gathering of trees, light danced through the leaves again. It shouldn't be there, as the clouds had rolled in, and yet sunny rays shimmered. Rian understood at once that his mother was with them. Stumbling over to the trees with Terra in his arms, he knelt to the Earth so the warm rays could dance across her skin.

"What do I do mother?" Rian whispered.

What's in your heart.

Rian looked down at Terra, a soul so pure and lovely that he could kick himself for ever having caused her an ounce of pain, and realized he would be nothing but an empty shell of a man without her by his side. How foolish he'd been to question for an instant the love that she offered so freely to him.

"Terra, my love. Terra, my heart. Terra, leader of Earth Fae, Goddess of my heart, I claim you a thousand times over. You, and only you, are my fated mate, and forever on, I will cherish you. Please, my love, hear my claim. Come back to me." Rian begged, whispering the words against her cheek, and was surprised to find tears wetting his cheeks. Light flashed, so brilliant that he had to close his eyes against it, and something inside him shifted. It was a subtle click, like a lock snapping into place, and liquid golden warmth filled him. His magick crowed, and he realized he was getting the rush of amplified powers that the Fae spoke about and so closely protected. In seconds, he twisted Terra in his arms and put his hands to her back, determined to heal her wound much like she'd once healed his.

So focused was he on pulling the dark poison from her body, that he barely noticed the others surround him and lay their hands on Terra. Together, they poured their love and magick into his woman, and, when Rian ripped the last nasty bit of dark magick from her and poured it into the ground, his entire body trembled with the effort.

"Rian." It was but a whisper, but it was all Rian needed to hear. Burying his head into her neck, he breathed a sigh of relief.

"Sweet Terra. My beautiful Goddess. You've come back to me."

"You claimed me." Terra gave a happy little trill. "I can feel it."

"I did, my love. It's an idiot I am for making you wait for my claim. I should have accepted you the moment you told me you were my fated mate."

"You can hold that over his head for ages now," Seamus piped up, and Terra chuckled, the vibrations of her laughter warming Rian.

"Oh, I plan to," Terra laughed, turning her head so her lips met his.

It was the kiss to end all kisses, and had they been anywhere else, at any other time, Rian would have sunk into it. Instead, he broke the kiss and looked up at the others.

"We need to leave at once. Be ready to transport as soon as possible."

"Where are we going?" Terra blinked up at him, her eyes still groggy with pain.

"I know just the spot," Rian promised her.

22

TERRA RESTED FOR A MOMENT, keeping her eyes closed and her head on Rian's shoulder, as he hurried the others along. It didn't really matter where they were going, so long as it was away from Goddess Domnu and the amulet came with her. Luckily, she could feel its happy hum at her leg. She had just been reaching for it when she'd been cornered by the Domnua, and now she was grateful to have it still strapped to her thigh. They were moving quickly, and it didn't matter if her pack got left behind. But not her...

Terra jerked her head up.

"Cormac." Instantly, sadness hit her like a ton of bricks, and tears began seeping from her eyes again. "We can't leave him."

"Shhh, darling, I'll take care of it. I promise you." Rian gave Callahan a look, who nodded once before crossing the meadow.

"Can he get him home?" Terra asked. She knew her brother was gone, at least from this realm, but still she wanted to perform his last rites. Though he'd left this world on a low note, his life hadn't been all bad. They would need to celebrate the whole of it, not just focusing on the distressing portions. Because wasn't that what life was about? Nobody was perfect all the time. A life was made up of mistakes and hurts and grievances, along with achievements, goodwill, and kind gestures. Terra refused to define her brother by the one devious act in his life but, at the same time, she could acknowledge that he'd done wrong. Either way, a life had ended, and he was due his last rites. She would perform them when she was able.

"Of course. Just focus on your healing, we'll take care of your brother." At the softness in his voice, Terra shifted and brought her hand to his face.

"You aren't angry with him anymore?" Terra studied her fated mate's perfect face.

"I don't know that it will go away that easily. It's not necessarily something I can immediately turn off, but I don't think he deserved death either. I may have said I wanted to kill him more than a few times during my exile, but it's not the justice I actually wanted served. I'm sorry for your loss," Rian said.

"That's fair," Terra said, pressing her lips together. She had to acknowledge Rian's feelings in all of this. Cormac had turned their lives upside down and would still do from his grave once her family learned of his misdeeds. But that was for another time, she supposed.

"Let's go," Bianca said, having hurried back with their satchels.

"Callahan?" Rian called across the meadow.

"It's done," Callahan said, and Terra closed her eyes in relief. "Cormac has returned home."

The guards would attend to his body, Terra knew from previous experiences when Fae returned to their realm after losing their lives. He was in safe hands now. Exhausted, Terra turned her face into Rian's chest and let the tears come.

The strange sucking sensation that went with transporting surrounded her, and, when it was over, Terra looked up and blinked. They were in another meadow, by another set of cliffs, and beside a cheerful looking cottage. A bark sounded, and Terra shifted to see a dog with ears flopping in the wind race over to them.

"That's a good girl. Haven't seen you in a bit, Rosie." Bianca crouched and scratched the dog's ears. Looking up at where Rian still held Terra, she smiled at him. "Good choice."

"Where are we?" Terra asked.

"At my home. I'm Gracie, by the way." A woman with tumbling hair and confident eyes nodded to Terra. "This wee beastie is my overly opinionated dog, and the lot of you are looking a touch worse for wear."

"A few bumps and bruises to heal up," Seamus said, brushing a kiss across Gracie's cheek.

"Well, come on in then. Let me see to it before you're on your way." Gracie said as Rian carried Terra inside the small cottage which smelled of lemon.

"I don't know that I need to be carried anymore," Terra protested, feeling just a touch silly in Rian's arms. She elbowed him until he let her feet slide to the floor, and then kept his arms around her as though he couldn't bear to let her go.

"You seem to have the most blood on you," Gracie said. She came to stand in front of Terra and held her hands out. "May I?"

"Of course," Terra said, instantly recognizing a healer. Her hands were cool to the touch, and Gracie closed her eyes as she focused inward for a moment.

"It smells divine in here," Bianca commented.

"Lemon curd. My mother's had a hankering for it," Gracie acknowledged. A cool wash of energy spilled through her, giving Terra a boost of strength, and she straightened, pleased with Gracie's work.

"That feels nice. Thank you, friend," Terra said with a small smile.

"Just clearing out the last dregs of dark magick. You would have cleared it out on your own soon enough, but no need to have it lingering. Is there anything to fear?" Gracie said, looking up at Rian as she moved to Bianca and ran her hands over where the blood matted at her scalp.

"Not here, no. I don't believe so at least. I think the Domnua will continue their battle in another realm." Rian's voice came from the floor where he'd crouched to give Rosie a cuddle after Gracie had given Terra the all clear. He looked positively kid-like, Terra realized, as he played with the dog, and she made a mental note to surprise Rian with a companion. It was clear his heart was crying out for love.

"You'll notify us if we need to protect ourselves?" Gracie asked. "We're not without our own power, here in

Grace's Cove. We'll do what we can to help. And to protect our people, of course."

"I'll send word, you know that Gracie," Bianca said, smiling when Gracie pulled her in for a quick hug. "I think we need to get back though. I don't even know where Goddess Domnu is right now, but I'm pretty sure she's furious we got away. We need to go to Callum."

"Ah, how's the lad doing then? Lily keeping him on his toes?"

"Are you kidding me? The man dotes on her. I'd say I was jealous, but I lucked out in that department, didn't I, lover?" Bianca winked at Seamus.

"Sure and it's me who has lucked out, isn't it then?" Seamus wrapped his arms around Bianca from behind and propped his chin on her head. Together, they rocked back and forth, and warmth filled Terra just looking at the love they had for each other.

"Let's skip the offer of tea then and we'll head down to the cove?" Gracie asked, pulling on a sweater that hung by a hook at the door.

"Oh but the lemon..." Bianca trailed off, her eyes hopeful.

"It's a shame, but it's still boiling. Gives you reason to come back for a proper visit." Gracie laughed when Bianca poked her lower lip out. Terra took one last glance around the pretty cottage, where a long table held a myriad jars and bowls, and shelves were stacked with a variety of natural ingredients. Kindred spirits, her and Gracie were, Terra realized and smiled.

"You heal with the Earth, too," Terra said, pointing at the shelves.

"I do at that. And with just a touch of power."

"The Earth Fae appreciate that. Blessed be," Terra bowed her head and walked outside to where the sea breeze sent a light shiver down her back. It wasn't unwelcome, the cold, for it kept her senses alert and reminded her how close she'd come to not feeling anything at all anymore. No, she'd welcome the cold and any other gifts the Earth would see fit to give her.

The couples walked, hand in hand, following Gracie across the meadow to where a picnic table sat by the edge of a cliff. Callahan followed at a slower pace behind them. At the top of the cliffs, Terra pulled up short and let out a small sigh of happiness. She'd only ever seen this cove from the beach, as that is where the Fae portal was hidden. From this viewpoint though? It was extraordinary. The cliffs hugged the calm blue water far below them, and birds played in the wind, dipping and diving toward the water on their hunt for fish. It was a space for dreamers and lovers alike, and Terra was instantly enchanted.

"This is where I'll say my goodbyes."

"What? Why?" Terra turned to where Callahan stood, arms crossed over his chest, newsboy cap pulled low on his forehead. "You'll come with us, of course. The Fire Fae are welcome."

"I understand and appreciate that, Lady Terra. But that realm isn't for me. I'll be staying right here."

"Are you certain? We can make your passage comfortable or ... right any wrongs, I'm sure of it," Terra said, carefully. She didn't know Callahan's past, but she could vouch for his actions toward her now. He'd be regaled as a hero by her people.

"Sure and I'm appreciating that. But, nevertheless, I'll be staying here."

"The house is yours to stay in. You have all the information you need to see that your needs are met?" Rian released Terra's hand and walked to Callahan.

"Of course. Thank you," Callahan tugged at the brim of his cap. "I'll be sure to handle any issues that arise at the company."

"Ah, they'll just replace me with the next bloodthirsty lot, I'm sure of it."

"Maybe, maybe not. You could change a few things there before you go. If you're wanting to, that is," Callahan offered. A considering look passed across Rian's face.

"You're not wrong. But you rarely ever are. Thank you, my friend, for being my guiding light when all I could see was darkness."

"You were worth saving."

The two men hugged, and Terra swiped at the tears that filled her eyes once more. Goodbyes were a part of life, but they still could hurt at times. Once everyone had said their farewells, Callahan turned and strode back across the meadow, whistling a merry tune. For a moment, Terra's eyes caught on the lonely figure.

"Will he be alright then?" Terra turned a worried look on Rian who looked dangerously close to tears himself.

"Callahan's like an alley cat. Lands on his feet. Don't mistake being alone for lonely. The man has a way of scrounging up company when he's in the mood and disappearing when he's not. Freedom is his favorite companion, and Ireland is his playground. I'll miss him — but I won't worry for him."

"I'll take your word for it," Terra smiled at Rian.

Together, the group descended the somewhat precarious path that hugged the rocky cliff wall, carefully picking their way down to the sandy beach at the bottom. Once there, Gracie paused them at the base of the cliffs.

"Typically, we'd do an offering here to give us safe passage onto the beach, but since you're with me, and mostly Fae, I don't think it will be needed," Gracie explained and stepped onto the sand. Terra was reminded that the cove was enchanted by more than just their own Fae wards to protect the portal.

The air shimmered in front of them, and Gracie skidded to a stop as Rosie barked at the air. In seconds, the shimmer dissolved to reveal Goddess Danu standing before them. Instantly, Terra bowed.

"My lady," Terra said, as the others took their cue and bowed to the Goddess of the Good Fae.

"Terra, Leader of Earth Fae, you've done well to bring the amulet back to your people. I am pleased to see my evil sister did not hurt you all."

"She killed my brother. Well, her people did," Terra said. The Goddess dropped her gaze, sadness crossing her beautiful features. Where Domnu was dark and edgy, Danula was soft and lovely in a shimmery gown of softest blue — like the sky at dawn.

"I am sorry for your loss. We'll help him on his passage through to the other realm," Goddess Danu promised. "I fear the worst is yet to come. Domnu is furious, and she'll only try twice as hard on her quest for domination now."

"Goddess." Bianca stepped forward and bobbed in an awkward little curtsey. "Lily and I have found a potential spell that might bind her powers. Is that … can you verify the truth of that?"

"There is a spell, yes." Goddess Danula pursed her lips as she thought of it. "It's an ancient one, but far stronger than any we've tried on her before. I'd forgotten the existence of it, truth be told."

"So … if all the parts align and we manage to follow the spell…?" Bianca asked, hope tinging her voice.

"We may see an end to Domnu's terror," Danula finished for Bianca.

"Brilliant," Bianca breathed and stepped backwards until once more she stood at Seamus's side.

"Rian, come forward." The Goddess beckoned to Rian, and he stepped forward, bowing his head once as she looked him up and down.

"Rian, Ruler of Magicks, exile of Earth Fae. You've shown yourself to be worthy of forgiveness. Though you've caused some damage in your quest for vengeance, I will task you with setting harms to right over the next few years." The Goddess steepled her fingers as she studied Rian.

"Of course. I had planned to anyway. I already have some ideas of what I can do to make up for some of the damage I've caused to the Earth."

"Lovely. I'll be watching that you do so. With that being said, I will also ask you for your forgiveness."

"My ... why?" Rian looked at the Goddess with a bewildered expression on his face.

"The Earth Fae wrongly punished you for a crime that was not your own. I should have tended to that, but I was called away on higher duties. I'm sorry for your suffering, but it seems it was all meant to be."

"Um, yes, of course. I forgive you." Rian said the words with a baffled look on his face. Terra didn't blame him. It wasn't often that a Goddess asked for forgiveness.

"Rian, you are relieved of your exile, as well as any past judgements held against you. You go home to your people a hero. With that being said, I have a gift to offer you. It isn't much, but I hope you will accept this in the sincere manner in which it is given."

The air shimmered once more, and Terra gasped when a figure appeared.

"Aster," Terra breathed.

"Mother!" Rian cried and stepped forward, stopping short of hugging her when he realized that she wasn't fully present.

"Your mother has crossed to the next realm, but I bring you her spirit so you may have the proper goodbye that you wished for." Goddess Danu stepped back a respectful distance to give the two space.

"Mother ... are you ... hurting still? Are you well?" Rian asked. The look on his face was enough to shred Terra's heart. She ached to go to him, but knew he needed to do this on his own.

"My darling boy, I am well. I feel no pain, which is the most important thing. What a weight has been lifted from my shoulders." Aster laughed and did a little jig on the beach. "Look at how well I can move now."

"I'm happy to see it," Rian said, his voice thick with emotion.

"I'm so glad you finally honored your word. My dear sweet boy — I'm so very proud of you. No matter what, I've always loved you, and will always love you. This love transcends realm and time, Rian. I'm always with you."

"I know it. You helped me ... with Terra. The light in the trees."

"Of course. I told you to look for me, didn't I? And it's a happy mother you've made me. What a lovely woman to have as your partner. Terra, you gave me great comfort in my last days. I'm honored you've chosen my boy as your mate."

"He's a good man. Even when he tried not to be. I'll take good care of him," Terra said, walking forward to wrap her arm around Rian's waist.

"See that you do. And you," Aster leveled a look at Rian. "No more of this vengeance nonsense. You've got a good woman to live for now. Take care of her and spend your days immersed in following the things that light you up inside. Those are the moments that matter. Always look for the light." Aster faded away.

Terra stood with Rian while he collected himself, grateful that the Goddess had given him this closure that he so desperately needed. It was nice to see that Aster was happy and no longer in pain, and she knew it would go a long way toward healing Rian's heart.

"The time has come to return. Your people await. I won't be far, as I fear, even know, that Domnu starts her war once more. Be well." With those final words, Goddess Danu faded away as well.

They stood in silence, simply appreciating the beauty of the waves lapping at the sand, processing the emotions of such a moment. Most people would never meet a Goddess in their lifetime, let alone more than one. The sheer intensity of their power and the magicks they held was enough to leave anyone awestruck.

Finally, Terra squeezed Rian's hand and started walking toward the narrow crevice in the cliff wall that would lead to the portal. Just before they stepped into the cave, a brilliant blue glow shone from the depths of the cove, and Terra gasped. Grabbing for Rian's hand, she laughed when his arms came around her.

"It shines in the presence of true love," Gracie explained, smiling at where the two couples were wrapped in each other's arms. "It's lucky you are, to have found each other. Not everyone does."

No, not everyone did. Terra thought of her brother with sadness. He would be a stark reminder for her to forever seek joy and treasure the love she had.

"And it's lucky I am not to have lost you," Rian said, turning her to claim her lips in a heated kiss. Pulling back, he smiled warmly at her as he brought her hands to his chest. "Goddess of my heart, I'll love you forever."

EPILOGUE

A SOFT HUMMING SOUND MET them as they walked across the meadow causing Rian to smile. It was the same sound that had greeted them when they'd first arrived home from the portal.

The trees were singing.

They did so whenever Terra was close, and he wondered if she even heard it anymore. The forest danced while she wandered through it, the flowers turning their faces to the sun, the trees waving their branches in greeting. All sorts of critters and wildlife would follow her, and he'd often catch her chatting with a butterfly, or scratching a rabbit behind its ear. The Earth loved Terra as much as she loved it, and though she'd told him to forgive himself, Rian still struggled with the shame that filled him when he thought back to how he'd been so careless with his actions toward the environment.

The world didn't need more polystyrene packaging. The world needed more people like Terra.

Rian had at least been able to rectify some of his wrongs, the latest just this morning. He'd crowed in delight when Callahan had sent along photos from where Rian had procured the forested land he had once ordered to be cleared. Rian had managed to wrest it away from the clutches of his prior company based on a loophole that he'd put into the contract for just such an occasion. Callahan had flown there to make sure the forest wasn't destroyed and was happy to report the orangutans were safe. Rian had even taken it a step further and had started the process of securing the paperwork to make the forest a protected space and would start building a sanctuary there for other orangutangs that had been exiled from their homes. Next up, he hoped to start a global education program about palm oil and the harmful practices used to manufacture it.

Terra's approving smile after he'd shown her the pictures of the orangutans was more than worth his efforts.

Rian was head over heels hopelessly in love. He was determined to spend every moment of every day protecting Terra, doting on her, and tending to their relationship with the same dedicated care that Terra took with nurturing the world around her. He'd been given a great gift, one that he could appreciate all the more for having experienced loss.

It was loss that took them to the woods this day.

Flower fairies flitted after them as they wound their way through the trees, a gentle breeze kissing their cheeks, the leaves rustling softly over their heads.

"Here it is, my love. See? Just like I told you." Terra

turned, concern in her eyes, and Rian found himself transfixed on her lovely face once more. He still couldn't quite believe that she was his. Going to her, Rian wrapped his arms around her waist and pulled her so her back nestled against his chest. Placing his chin on her head, he breathed in her refreshing scent, and studied the bush she'd planted for his mother when Aster had passed. It had been over two years now since his mother had died, and the bush had grown from a small plant to a thriving shrub.

"Buckthorn," Terra said, and then pointed to where Aster flowers also bloomed along the riverbank.

"And asters. Buckthorn for the butterflies and bees and asters for my mother." Rian could think of his mother now without tears welling. Instead he found peace in knowing that Terra was with her at the end of her days. The flower fairies danced across the shrub, and golden tendrils flitted from their wings, curling among the leaves. Sunlight split the canopy above them and shimmered across the forest floor.

"Where the sun shines through the trees, blessing the ground with light, I will always be. Remember me and I will come to you," Rian murmured, pressing his lips to Terra's head. "This is a perfect spot, Terra. Thank you for doing this for my mother."

"It's sorry I am that you didn't get to spend her final days together, but at the very least you'll have a nice spot to visit and reminisce." Terra patted his arms that circled her waist, and he tightened his grip on her. Twisting, she looked up at him. "Are you sure you want to come with me for the next part?"

"Of course, Terra. I'm always going to support you. This is important," Rian said. He released Terra, but not before dropping a quick kiss to her lips, and then threaded his fingers through hers as they wandered farther up the stream until they came to a spot that Terra had picked. "Which bush did you decide upon?"

"An elder bush," Terra said. She pursed her lips as they came to a stop by where a guard had brought out a shovel and a bush ready for planting. "It has several meanings, depending on which history you look at. The Fae believe it to keep evil spirits away. The humans who follow Christianity believe it to be a traitor bush from one of their stories. I thought the mixed meanings to be appropriate here, though for me, no plant carries bad meanings. Just various ways it contributes to the environment as a whole."

"I think it is the perfect choice for Cormac," Rian said, and hefted the shovel. With Terra directing, Rian dug a hole to plant a bush for the man who had betrayed them both. He no longer felt anger for Cormac, though he wouldn't necessarily look back on the man fondly either. Once the hole was deep enough, he waited for Terra to direct him.

Today she wore a gold dress, similar to the one she'd worn on their first date, with green leaves etched at the hem. A gilded crown pulled her hair back from her face, and her green eyes were luminous as she lifted a golden urn. Terra stepped forward until she stood just at the edge of the river and bowed her head in silence. When she lifted it, a beam of light speared the branches, illuminating her, and she uncovered the urn. Bending, Terra tilted the urn until the ashes inside sprinkled into the water that rushed past.

"From dust to ashes, and back again, our soul reunites with its home — the Earth from whence it came. It's no more a goodbye than it is a welcoming, and our Earth greets our brother with great joy, quiet acceptance, and resounding love as Cormac's ashes return to the Earth to take root once more with our future brethren," Terra said, her voice ringing across the forest. The trees raised their song, a resounding chorus, as Cormac's ashes returned to the Earth.

"A chorus of ashes," Rian murmured, understanding dawning about the role the trees played in the Earth Fae's world. It was all interconnected, soulful energy uniting, and it now made sense why Aster had directed him to look for her among the trees.

"It is, indeed. A beautiful one at that," Terra said, turning to smile up at where the branches waved above them as though the trees had raised their arms to the sky in praise. "Let's plant, shall we?"

"Of course," Rian said. He lifted the bush and positioned it in the middle of the hole while Terra worked quietly to fill in the dirt on the sides of the roots. They did so in silence, seeming to understand that both would have their own feelings about honoring Cormac's memory. When she finished, Terra stood and brushed the dirt from her hands, tears shining in her eyes.

The song of the trees reached a crescendo.

"I'm sorry he hurt you," Rian said, pulling Terra into his arms. He hated seeing the tears in her eyes.

"Oh, goddess, but I should be the one apologizing to

you," Terra sighed. "But today isn't for apologies, not really. We've said all those. Today is about forgiveness and honoring the life of a flawed man. Nobody is perfect, but he paid the ultimate sacrifice in trying to right his wrongs."

"For which I am forever grateful," Rian said, rocking Terra gently in his arms as the trees finished their song.

"Farewell, my brother. You'll be missed."

They stood like that, listening to the music of the trees, and watching as the forest animals came past to pay their respects. Eventually, Terra shifted in his arms, and pulled away, reaching for his hand once more.

"Come, Rian. I have a surprise for you."

"For me? Whatever for?" Rian asked, immediately suspicious. He dearly hoped it wasn't something formal with King Callum like being knighted or something of that nature. Though he'd been offered his Head of Magicks role again when they'd first arrived back to the Fae realm, Rian had refused it in order to be available for Terra's needs. They both knew another battle loomed, and Rian wasn't about to let Terra head off to war or whatever may come without him by her side. He'd already almost lost her once, it wasn't about to happen again. At least not on his watch.

"Because I love you," Terra said, smiling up at him. "Because I wanted to do something nice for you. Because I love seeing your smile come more easily these days. For a while I was certain your face had frozen into a glower." Terra pulled a sullen face, trying to mimic Rian's angry expression he once wore regularly, and he grinned despite himself.

"Yes, well, now I have something to smile about. Particularly when you..." Rian leaned down and whispered about a naughty move Terra had performed on him the night before when they'd been alone together. Pink flushed Terra's cheeks, and she bit her lip, making him instantly want her once more.

Now was certainly not the time for such a thing, Rian reminded his baser self, and pushed those thoughts aside as they neared a clearing in the meadow where a royal guard stood holding a large wicker basket. At Terra's nod, he placed the basket on the ground and disappeared from the field.

"Are we having a picnic?" Rian asked. "Sure and that's a nice surprise. Thank you, Terra."

"No we aren't having a picnic." Terra rolled her eyes and tugged him to the basket. "But I should have known food would be the way to cheering you up. No, this is something else. I ... well, I guess you'll see. I just thought you might—"

"Careful," Rian warned, grabbing Terra, and pulling her backward as the basket shook.

"I promise you, it's not dangerous." Terra laughed. "Well, perhaps to your heart."

Rian's mouth dropped open as the basket toppled over and an enthusiastic puppy bounded out. He was already dropping to his knees to catch the blur of fur and energy as it lapped enthusiastically at his face.

"A puppy?" Rian breathed, his heart splitting open at the fuzzball that shook with delight in his arms. "You got me a puppy?"

"I did, at that. You seemed to love Rosie so much, and

it was the first time that I'd ever seen you so ... I don't know. Just relaxed? Captivated? Childlike?" Terra tapped a finger on her lips as she thought about it. "Or maybe it was just because you'd let your guard down and genuinely looked happy. I thought ... well, why not? The man deserves a puppy. And don't worry — I've already spoken to my parents about when we have to attend to royal duties. They are on full puppy watch. In fact, I barely pulled this rascal away from my father."

Terra and her parents had managed to repair their relationship after news of Cormac's betrayal and subsequent death had made it home. Eoghan had delivered a heartfelt and prompt apology to Terra, and they'd been working on mending their shared hurts since. Rian wasn't sure what would come of Eoghan's relationship with his wife, but that, at least, wasn't a problem for Rian to solve.

"I get to keep him?" Disbelief filled Rian as the puppy rolled over on its back, pawing the air, while it looked up at him with a smile on its face. "What does he want?"

"I think he wants you to scratch his tummy. And yes, you get to keep him." Terra chuckled. "What's his name?"

"Callahan," Rian said immediately, and Terra laughed again and dropped to the grass next to him.

"A mighty name for a mighty wee beastie," Terra agreed, giggling as the puppy tumbled its way over to her.

Rian's heart was full. It didn't matter the future they faced, or the fights they would fight, because nothing could take from him this moment in time full of love and laughter. It was like capturing sunshine in a bottle. It was just as his mother had promised him, and Rian held tightly to that thought now. Whatever darkness came, he'd always look for the light among the leaves.

Don't worry! Even though Rian insists his friend Callahan (not his new puppy!) is happy on his own, you can still read about Callahan's second chance at love in this bonus scene: Go to
www.triciaomalley.com/free
to download
Chorus of Ashes: Callahan's Love.

LYRIC OF WIND

BOOK 4 IN THE WILDSONG SERIES

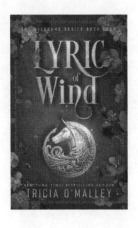

"You have to come down at some point," Alistair, Kellen's best friend and second-in-command called to him from where they raced their steeds on the wind. As Air Fae, they commanded the skies, and alicorns were their chariots of choice. Winged unicorns, both fierce and loyal, the alicorns loved nothing more than to stretch their wings in a good race.

"Make me," Kellen challenged, urging his beast on. He laughed as the alicorn dove, catching the wind, dipping among the clouds. Kellen's heart soared, as he was always at his most free when he was riding the wind, and not stuck in royal court dealing with the minutiae of day-to-day royal duties that his father insisted he handle.

Even though he'd stepped into power as leader of the Air Fae over a year ago, his father, Devlin, acted as though he'd been the one chosen for the role instead of Kellen. Once Kellen had been instated, Devlin had shouldered his way into almost every meeting and decision that had been thrust upon Kellen, acting as though he had the right to make choices in matters that didn't pertain to him. They'd gone many a round about it, and yet, *still*, his father refused to listen to Kellen's requests that he stay out of Royal Fae business.

His father's actions were causing ripples of distrust through the Air Fae, and many were starting to question the choice of Kellen as a ruler. Now, Devlin's latest campaign —for Kellen to claim his fated mate — had sent Kellen to the skies to escape.

His fated mate.

Like he didn't have bigger things to worry about?

Not only was Kellen new to this position, but he was beginning to chafe at the responsibilities that came with being a leader. Each day ended with a headache from one problem or another, and Kellen was starting to believe that maybe the people were right. Maybe he wasn't suited to being their ruler.

And now his father called for him to find his fated mate. It was like Devlin just wanted to heap one more problem on top of his already growing pile of issues to deal with. Was the man trying to test his limits?

Or was he just jealous?

Kellen's thoughts froze when Alistair screamed, blood blooming on his chest, and tumbled from the back of his steed. Already Kellen was diving, urging his alicorn on, and still he wasn't sure he'd make it before Alistair hit the ground. He didn't chance looking over his shoulder at what had dared enter their sacred space and attack. If he broke his focus for even half a second, Alistair would be gone.

As the ground screamed toward them, Kellen closed his eyes and pulled at his magick, whispering an incantation that he prayed would save his friend in time.

Order Lyric of Wind today!

THE ISLE OF DESTINY SERIES
ALSO BY TRICIA O'MALLEY

Do you want to learn more about how Bianca & Seamus fell in love and helped battle the Dark Fae during the Four Treasures quest? Read the complete Isle of Destiny series in Kindle Unlimited!

Stone Song

Sword Song

Spear Song

Sphere Song

A completed series.

Available in audio, e-book & paperback!

"Love this series. I will read this multiple times. Keeps you on the edge of your seat. It has action, excitement and romance all in one series."

- Amazon Review

WILD SCOTTISH KNIGHT

BOOK 1 IN THE ENCHANTED HIGHLANDS SERIES

Opposites attract in this modern-day fairytale when American, Sophie MacKnight, inherits a Scottish castle along with a hot grumpy Scotsman who is tasked with training her to be a magickal knight to save the people of Loren Brae.

A brand new series from Tricia O'Malley.
Pre-Order Wild Scottish Knight today.

THE WILDSONG SERIES
ALSO BY TRICIA O'MALLEY

Song of the Fae

Melody of Flame

Chorus of Ashes

Lyric of Wind

"The magic of Fae is so believable. I read these books in one sitting and can't wait for the next one. These are books you will reread many times."

- Amazon Review

Available in audio, e-book & paperback!

Available Now

THE SIREN ISLAND SERIES
ALSO BY TRICIA O'MALLEY

Good Girl

Up to No Good

A Good Chance

Good Moon Rising

Too Good to Be True

A Good Soul

In Good Time

A completed series.

Available in audio, e-book & paperback!

"Love her books and was excited for a totally new and different one! Once again, she did NOT disappoint! Magical in multiple ways and on multiple levels. Her writing style, while similar to that of Nora Roberts, kicks it up a notch!! I want to visit that island, stay in the B&B and meet the gals who run it! The characters are THAT real!!!" - Amazon Review

THE ALTHEA ROSE SERIES
ALSO BY TRICIA O'MALLEY

One Tequila

Tequila for Two

Tequila Will Kill Ya (Novella)

Three Tequilas

Tequila Shots & Valentine Knots (Novella)

Tequila Four

A Fifth of Tequila

A Sixer of Tequila

Seven Deadly Tequilas

Eight Ways to Tequila

Tequila for Christmas (Novella)

"Not my usual genre but couldn't resist the Florida Keys setting. I was hooked from the first page. A fun read with just the right amount of crazy! Will definitely follow this series."- Amazon Review

A completed series.

Available in audio, e-book & paperback!

THE MYSTIC COVE SERIES

Wild Irish Heart

Wild Irish Eyes

Wild Irish Soul

Wild Irish Rebel

Wild Irish Roots: Margaret & Sean

Wild Irish Witch

Wild Irish Grace

Wild Irish Dreamer

Wild Irish Christmas (Novella)

Wild Irish Sage

Wild Irish Renegade

Wild Irish Moon

"I have read thousands of books and a fair percentage have been romances. Until I read Wild Irish Heart, I never had a book actually make me believe in love."- Amazon Review

A completed series.

Available in audio, e-book & paperback!

ALSO BY TRICIA O'MALLEY

STAND ALONE NOVELS

<u>Ms. Bitch</u>

"Ms. Bitch is sunshine in a book! An uplifting story of fighting your way through heartbreak and making your own version of happily-ever-after."

~Ann Charles, USA Today Bestselling Author

<u>Starting Over Scottish</u>

Grumpy. Meet Sunshine.

She's American. He's Scottish. She's looking for a fresh start. He's returning to rediscover his roots.

<u>One Way Ticket</u>

A funny and captivating beach read where booking a one-way ticket to paradise means starting over, letting go, and taking a chance on love...one more time

10 out of 10 - The BookLife Prize

AFTERWORD

Thank you to my fantastic editors, beta readers, and husband who are always there to help make my stories shine. It takes a village, and thank you for being a part of mine.

As always, a huge thank you to, *you*, my amazing reader, for continuing to take a chance on my books. I say it all the time, but I really do have the best readers in the world.

Sparkle on!

CONTACT ME

I hope my books have added a little magick into your life. If you have a moment to add some to my day, you can help by telling your friends and leaving a review. Word-of-mouth is the most powerful way to share my stories. Thank you.

Love books? What about fun giveaways? Nope? Okay, can I entice you with underwater photos and cute dogs? Let's stay friends, receive my emails and contact me by signing up at my website

www.triciaomalley.com

Or find me on Facebook and Instagram.
@triciaomalleyauthor

Made in the USA
Las Vegas, NV
08 November 2023

80434617R00152